KT-502-911

PUFFIN B

Echo Come Home

Praise for Megan Rix

'If you love Michael Morpurgo, you'll enjoy this' *Sunday Express*

'A moving tale told with warmth, kindliness and lashings of good sense that lovers of Dick King-Smith will especially appreciate' *The Times*

'Every now and then a writer comes along with a unique way of storytelling. Meet Megan Rix . . . her novels are deeply moving and will strike a chord with animal lovers' *LoveReading*

'A perfect story for animal lovers and lovers of adventure stories' *Travelling Book Company*

Praise from Megan's young readers

'I never liked reading until one day I was in Waterstones and I picked up some books. One was . . . called *The Bomber Dog*. I loved it so much I couldn't put it down' Luke, 8

'I found this book amazing' Nayah, 11

'EPIC BOOK!!!' Jessica, 13

'One of my favourite books' Chloe, Year 8

MEGAN RIX is the recent winner of the Stockton and Shrewsbury Children's Book Awards, and has been shortlisted for numerous other children's book awards. She lives with her husband by a river in England. When she's not writing, she can be found walking her golden retrievers, Traffy and Bella, who are often in the river.

Books by Megan Rix

THE BOMBER DOG

THE GREAT ESCAPE

THE HERO PUP

THE RUNAWAYS

A SOLDIER'S FRIEND

THE VICTORY DOGS

www.meganrix.com

Echo Come Home

megan rix

PUFFIN

PUFFIN BOOKS

UK | USA | Canada | Ireland | Australia
India | New Zealand | South Africa

Puffin Books is part of the Penguin Random House group of companies
whose addresses can be found at global.penguinrandomhouse.com.

puffinbooks.com

First published 2016
001

Text copyright © Megan Rix, 2016

The moral right of the author has been asserted

Set in 13/20 pt Baskerville MT Std
Typeset by Jouve (UK), Milton Keynes
Printed in Great Britain by Clays Ltd, St Ives plc

A CIP catalogue record for this book is available from the British Library

ISBN: 978–0–141–35766–9

www.greenpenguin.co.uk

Penguin Random House is committed to a
sustainable future for our business, our readers
and our planet. This book is made from Forest
Stewardship Council® certified paper.

Every dog has his day . . .

Chapter 1

Jake watched the shaggy-coated little dog through the supermarket window as he waited for his mum and younger sister, Vicky, to fetch a trolley. The dog wagged its tail every time someone dropped a coin into the homeless man's cap. Jake smiled. It was almost like the little dog was saying thank you.

'Excuse me,' a voice behind Jake said, but Jake didn't move. 'Excuse me!' the voice repeated more loudly. Finally, the man shook his head and pushed his trolley round the boy.

Eleven-year-old Jake didn't realize that he was standing in people's way by the door and he was oblivious to the black looks he was getting from shoppers trying to get past him with their trolleys.

He wished he had a dog. A dog that would spend all day with him and always be there for him, like the homeless man's dog was.

'Excuse me . . . you're in my way . . . Can you just move . . . for goodness' sake!'

Jake turned in surprise as a trolley bumped into the back of him. He stared at the shopper's angry face. Her lips opened and closed as she spoke.

'. . . rude boy . . .' he lip-read, before the woman bustled on into the supermarket.

Jake flinched and his face burned red as he turned back to look at the dog. Now it was sitting on the pavement next to the old homeless man. It held its paw out to Jake's mum and eight-year-old Vicky.

'Spare a few coins, lady?' said the homeless man.

The little grizzle-coated terrier cross stood up and wagged his tail. His head tilted to one side as he looked up at them. Jake watched his mum drop some coins into the man's cap.

'Thank you kindly,' Jake lip-read.

'Jake!' Vicky yelled, when she saw her brother through the glass.

'Shh, Vicky,' her mum said. 'You know he can't hear you.'

'Why didn't he wait for us to get the trolley? He's always wandering off and then we have to chase after him,' Vicky grumbled. 'He can be a right pain sometimes.'

Once they'd gone, the homeless man took the coins out of his cap and put them in his pocket. He grinned at the little dog. 'You bring old George luck, you do, Bones,' he said.

The little dog's tail wagged.

'Afternoon, George,' a young man in a brown suit said, coming over to them. 'Lovely day.'

'Can't complain,' George said, as he tugged at the tattered red-and-white spotted bandana he liked to wear round his neck. It was very warm for March.

'How've you been keeping?'

'Not too bad, Mr C. Can't complain.'

He knew Charles Cooper from way back. The first time they'd met, Mr C, as everyone called him, had been a student running the food bank. George hadn't seen him for a while though, not since he'd dished up the roast potatoes at the Christmas lunch for the homeless they had every year at the town hall. George still thought about those potatoes. He'd even dreamt about them once.

'Heard you'd been promoted,' George said.

Mr Cooper nodded. 'I'm going to be running the Fresh Start Hostel over by the park. You

4

should come and see how the building work's progressing, George. The place is going to be fit for a king once it's done.'

But George wasn't even sure he wanted to live at the hostel yet. He didn't like the thought of all those walls closing in around him. Or of the doors trapping him in at night. He wanted to be free to come and go as he pleased, especially when the weather was warm like today. Although in the winter, when the nights grew bitter and his bones ached from the cold, maybe a hostel wouldn't be such a bad place to live. It'd be warm and Mr C would make sure there was always plenty to eat. Maybe even dish up some of those roast potatoes.

'That your dog, George?' Mr Cooper asked him.

George shook his head. 'He's not anyone's dog but his own. I call him Bones because I get him one from the butcher's when I can. Bones loves his bones.'

Mr Cooper reached over to stroke the dog, but Bones backed away.

'Doesn't like to be stroked,' George said, as the young man tried to coax the dog to him. 'At least not until he gets to know you, and sometimes not even then.'

'Why not?' Mr Cooper asked. But George didn't know the answer to that.

From a safe distance the little dog looked up at him with his big brown eyes and wagged his tail.

'Having him around reminds me of what it used to be like,' George said softly, almost to himself.

'What used to be like?'

'Having a home and someone who cares about you.'

'You could have that again once the new hostel opens in the summer. All it takes is that first step. There's going to be a festival in the park to celebrate its opening and raise funds

6

to keep it running. I'm on my way to help design the posters for it now.'

George's watery, tired blue eyes looked up at Mr Cooper. He'd had enough of hearing about the hostel.

'Spare a bit of change, guv? For the dog,' he said.

Mr Cooper sighed and dropped some coins into George's cap.

Bones came back to George once Mr C had gone.

'I wish I could give you a proper home,' the old man said. 'You deserve somewhere warm and safe with lots of good food.' He didn't know if the Fresh Start Hostel would allow pets or not, but most places didn't.

The little dog whined and put out his paw.

'Well, at least we'll both have something nice to eat today and some for the others, too,' George said. He groaned as he stood up and headed off down the street with Bones trotting along beside him.

First they went to the butcher's to get a bone and then they visited the fish and chip shop.

'As many chips as this'll buy,' George said, as he emptied his pockets of all the coins they'd collected.

Mandy looked over at the little dog waiting for George outside the door. It reminded her of the dog she'd had when she was a little girl. As a special treat, she gave George far more chips than his money would normally have bought.

'There you go,' she said. 'I put a bit of leftover fish in there too. And this is for your dog.' She held out a saveloy.

'Thank you.'

George took the saveloy from her, scooped up the hot bags of chips and fish from the counter and headed out of the shop.

Mandy watched through the window as the little dog wolfed down the saveloy in a few big gulps. George gave her a thumbs up and she waved back.

'Come on, Bones,' George said.

He didn't hear the swish of the skateboard's wheels as it headed along the pavement, but Bones did and he gave a bark. George looked round just in time and was able to step back before the skateboard and its rider ran into him.

'Thank you,' George said to Bones. It wasn't the first time the little dog had alerted him to something that he hadn't heard coming.

The two of them walked down to the river on the outskirts of town. Under the bridge other homeless people gathered at night for shelter and company.

The chips weren't hot by the time George and Bones arrived, but they weren't cold either, and everyone was grateful as George handed round the delicious salty fried potatoes and leftover fish.

'There you go, Mike . . . This is for you, Jen . . . Here you are, Harvey . . . Cole, Blue . . . Jay, Kel . . .'

The little dog lay down on the muddy ground beneath the bridge and started gnawing on his bone.

'Always get more money when he's with me,' George said, as the rest of them ate.

'Got more in one day than I usually get in a week when he spent the day with me,' Jen agreed.

'Missed him when he took himself off,' said Harvey, as he ate his chips with one hand and sketched the dog on the paper the chips had been wrapped in with the other. Bones had been gone for weeks and none of them knew where he'd disappeared to, just like they didn't know where he'd come from when he first turned up. A little dog without a collar and a fear of being stroked, at least until he got to know you, and sometimes not even then.

They were all glad when he'd come back home to the bridge and not just because of the increase in the money they could collect. Everyone felt happier when Bones was around, but they knew he could take off at any moment. He didn't belong to anyone.

'Never known a dog to dislike being stroked before,' Mike said.

'Something bad must have happened,' said George, and the others nodded.

As it grew darker, the people who lived under the bridge settled down for the night. For the moment it served as a windbreak and an umbrella from the rain, but the bridge was condemned and none of them knew how long it would be before it was taken down meaning they would lose the only home they had.

*

As the sun came up, Bones yawned, blinked and stretched out his legs all the way to the ends of his paws. He rolled over on to his back with his legs in the air, then rolled on to his other side, stood up and gave himself a shake.

The earth beneath the condemned bridge was hard, cold and often damp. But he'd nestled close to George and shared his body warmth. With the rough blanket, cardboard-box mattress and a full belly, they'd both been able to sleep pretty well.

'Don't go, Bones,' George said sleepily. But Bones was already heading off.

The scaffolding supporting the crumbling bridge stopped people from using it as a shortcut into town, but it was no obstacle for the little dog. His claws made tapping noises as he nimbly crossed the steel structure before jumping on to the soft, overgrown grass on the other side.

His short tail was held confidently high as he trotted along beside the river, past the quacking ducks and gliding swans.

'Morning, dog,' one of the night fishermen called to him, as he tossed Bones a crust from the remains of his ham sandwich. It was gulped down in a second and Bones wagged his tail as he looked cheekily over at the bag the sandwich had come from and then back at the man.

'That's all there is left,' the night fisherman told the dog, as he packed up his fishing tackle. 'Time I was heading home.' But when he looked round the little dog had already gone.

Bones didn't follow the route into the town centre that everyone else took. His was a lot quicker. Under the broken gate of number 23, into the back garden of number 9 with the sheets hanging on the line, across the churchyard, avoiding the gardener who'd once thrown a bit of broken brick at him, and through the car park, keeping a careful lookout for cars.

A cat jumped up on to a wall as he ran into the park. But Bones never chased cats, or squirrels, like a pet dog might do.

He crossed the park and stopped at the pelican crossing of a busy main road and sat down. He didn't have long to wait.

'Hello there,' a woman, heading off to work, said. She reached out a hand to stroke him, but he took a few steps back so she couldn't reach him.

The woman pressed the crossing button and as soon as the beeps started Bones ran across the road. Ahead of him lay the town centre.

The early-morning roadsweeper stopped pushing his handcart.

'Here you go, Muttley,' he said, throwing a half-eaten burger he'd just picked up to the dog.

Bones swallowed it down and then looked up at the roadsweeper and gave a wag of his tail. The man pushed his cart further up the street as Bones trotted on too.

The hamburger was good, but best of all was the street where the takeaway food restaurants were. Bones's pace quickened as he got closer. Most days there was a little food lying on the ground at whatever time he got there. But on one day every week, one special day, the restaurants put out all their bins filled with tempting delicacies for the people in big trucks to take away. And today was that day.

'Here, dog . . .' Boris from Freddy's Fried Chicken said, throwing Bones some leftovers.

Boris didn't know what the dog's real name was or even if he had one, but he felt sorry for the stray and had started to leave a small plastic tub of fresh water out for him. He'd tried to stroke the dog, but it wouldn't let him get close enough to do so. Boris missed his own dog who was still living at his parents' home while Boris studied at university.

Bones gulped down the chicken before heading past The Golden Elephant, Pizza Perfect and The Curry Stop.

As soon as he'd gone, Boris pressed the dog warden's number into his mobile phone.

'That little dog's here again,' he said. 'It's definitely a stray.'

'I'm in the van and on my way,' the dog warden told him.

She'd had more than one phone call reporting this particular stray in the last few weeks. But so far she hadn't been able to catch him. The little dog was just too quick and as soon as he heard her coming he was off. She was determined that he wasn't going to escape again today.

Bones stopped at The Blue Lotus on the corner. As usual, seventeen-year-old Li had a paper carton of leftover fried noodles waiting for him. The little dog wagged his tail as Li put the carton down on the ground. But he waited until Li stepped back before putting his head into the carton and starting to eat.

'You are one noodle-loving dog,' Li said as he watched him slurping down the noodles.

Li pulled his phone from his pocket and took a photo of Bones eating.

'I'm going to put this on the internet,' he said, grinning at the photo he'd taken. The little dog had noodles hanging from his mouth and a look of pure pleasure in his eyes.

'It's not like he's being a nuisance or anything, but that dog shouldn't be living on the streets,' Jay from Pizza Perfect told the dog warden when she arrived. He pointed towards The Blue Lotus.

'What if he got run over?' the chef from The Golden Elephant said, as he watched the dog warden take the dog-catching net from the back of her van. 'And a dog shouldn't live on takeaway food, should it? It can't be good for him.'

The dog warden nodded: that little dog wasn't going to get away today. Her mouth was set firm as she grasped the net and crept down the street.

Bones's head was down as he licked up the very last bite of the noodles. He didn't see the dog warden advancing silently down the street towards him, but he did hear her when her foot stepped on an empty box. He looked round and saw the dog-catching net raised high to swoop down on him. The net hit the ground empty as Bones scampered off down the street.

'Quick, stop him!' the dog warden shouted at Li.

But it was too late. The little dog was racing past The Curry Stop, Perfect Pizza and The Golden Elephant.

The dog warden might never have caught him had Boris not got in the way.

'Stop that dog!' the dog warden yelled.

Boris tried to grab him and, as the little dog dodged away from his hands, the dog-catching net landed on top of him.

'Gotcha!'

Chapter 2

There were several dog crates inside the dog warden's van, but no other dogs.

'In you go,' the dog warden said, and she lifted up the fold-over bolts on the top of the nearest crate and put the squirming dog inside.

'There's no point making all that fuss,' she said, as the little dog immediately started to bark, paw and bite at the bars.

She shook her head as she headed round to the front of the van, pulled off her thick, dog-bite protection gloves and started the engine. By the time she drove off, Bones had stopped biting at the bars and was looking up at the bolts on the top of the crate instead.

The back of the dog warden's van didn't have any windows so Bones couldn't see out. But he heard the sound of children calling to each other in a school playground as they drove past.

Jake didn't play with the other children before school or at breaktimes. Instead he spent his time standing alone by the iron railings that went all the way round the playground, looking out. He saw the dog warden's van, with the painted pawprints on the side, drive past. He wished he could be in it, speeding off somewhere. Anywhere other than school would be fine.

He rubbed at his tired eyes and yawned. People thought when you couldn't hear that you just existed in a world of silence, like you were living at the bottom of a well. But it wasn't like that for Jake, although sometimes he wished it were. He might not be able to hear what was going on around him, but his head was sometimes so full of whistling, hissing or drilling sounds that they drowned out all other noises and made it very hard to concentrate and almost impossible to sleep at night.

The noise in his head was called tinnitus. Jake tried to ignore it, but sometimes that was really difficult and it kept him awake. Even putting a pillow over his ears and pressing down hard didn't stop it.

When he was five, Jake had contracted meningitis, which left him with severe hearing loss in both ears. With his hearing aids in, he could follow a conversation so long as there wasn't much background noise, but if there was then he had to rely on lip-reading to help him understand.

It had been different at his old school. Everyone there knew him before he was deaf, and he'd had a communication support worker called Maxine to help him. She'd made sure he didn't fall behind in his schoolwork as well as helping him learn sign language and how to lip-read.

When they moved to the other side of town, Jake and his sister Vicky had started at a new school and everything had changed. There was no communication support worker to repeat what the teacher said if Jake hadn't understood the first time and so keeping up was much harder.

It was all right for Vicky. She loved their new school and had made tons of friends in no time at all. But he hadn't.

When Jake looked back, the other children were already heading inside. The bell must have rung. High-pitched sounds were much harder for him to hear than lower noises.

Jake pushed his hands deep into his pockets and followed them.

He could tell whether the other children were laughing or shouting at each other by the expressions on their faces and body language. If they kept still, and he looked at their lips, he could lip-read what they were saying. But he didn't like looking at other people. So he stared down at his own feet instead, not catching anyone's eye.

'Morning, Jake,' a red-headed boy called Tony said, as Jake made his way across the classroom, but Jake didn't look round because he hadn't heard him.

He sat by himself at a double desk at the front, concentrating hard on the teacher's lips as she took the register. To make sure he didn't miss what the teacher said, he had to watch her lips all the time as well as hear some of what she said with his hearing aids.

Some of the letters appeared very similar to each other when he tried to lip-read them. The letters 'P' and 'B' looked almost the same and numbers were particularly tricky.

'Tony Mills,' Miss Dawson read out, and Jake looked over as Tony, two rows back, put his hand up.

'Here, miss.'

It was easy to lip-read the names of the other children in the class when the teacher kept her head up. But when she looked down at the register, or held it in front of her face instead, it was just about impossible.

'Sanjay d'Silva?'

'Here, miss.'

'Meena Nawaz?'

'Here, miss.'

'Amos Jones?'

'Here, miss.'

'Chloe Cartwright?'

'Here, miss.'

'Jake Logan?'

Miss Dawson looked over at Jake.

'Jake Logan,' she repeated, as she lowered the register so he could see her lips.

'Here, miss,' Jake said.

Although the truth was he wished he weren't there. He wished he didn't have to go to school. He wished the second hand of the clock on the wall weren't so slow. At least it was Friday.

By the time the dog warden pulled up at the animal rescue centre, Bones wasn't in the crate she'd put him in any more. The little Border terrier cross wasn't the first dog to have escaped from a dog crate and the warden was ready with her thick gloves on and caught him as he tried to jump out of the van.

'We should call you Little Houdini,' she said, chuckling, as Karen, who ran the rescue centre, came to join her. 'He's one smart dog. I've had reports of him for weeks, but it took until today to catch him.'

'Definitely Border terrier, judging by his overgrown coat, but I'm not sure what he's crossed with,' Karen said, as she noted Bones's bright eyes and white teeth. 'He's not very old. Not even two I'd say. Just a puppy really.'

'A very dirty puppy,' said the dog warden, as the little dog looked up at her.

Karen nodded. 'His fur's really thick and matted. He'll feel so much better once I've given him a good bath and a haircut. Do you think he's been microchipped?'

The dog warden shook her head. 'Seems like too much of a stray,' she said. 'But still worth giving it a go.'

Karen ran the microchip detector over the nape of Bones's neck where the microchip should be and then over the rest of his back in case it had slipped. Nothing showed up on the screen.

'Just as I thought,' the dog warden said.

'Rehoming in seven days then,' said Karen. 'Only . . .'

'What?'

'Lenny from Helper Dogs is coming over tomorrow. I'd like to show this little chap to him, unless his owner comes forward before then, of course.'

'Can't hurt.'

'Seems a shame not to – after all, he's not likely to be claimed and Lenny might want him,' Karen said.

The dog warden's phone rang. This time it was someone complaining about a noisy dog. She was still talking on the phone as she went out to her van with a wave and a thumbs up to Karen.

'Right, Little Houdini,' Karen said, once the dog warden had gone. 'Time for a bath.' She put on a waterproof apron, because dog bathing could involve a lot of splashing, and picked up a muzzle. As soon as he saw it, Bones turned his head away. But he really didn't have a choice.

'That's it,' Karen said, once the muzzle was over his mouth and secure. The little dog stared at her in utter misery, but he had to be bathed and that was that. Some dogs loved water, but others hated it, or just didn't like being clean, and Karen didn't want to get off on the wrong foot with Little Houdini by putting him in a situation where he panicked and tried to bite her.

Nevertheless the little dog's body trembled with fear and she could feel his heart racing as she lifted him into the metal dog bath.

'Hush now, it's OK,' Karen said, as she turned on the water and lifted the shower hose. But Bones didn't stop shaking.

'It's not that bad,' Karen said, trying to calm him down, as she ran warm water over his coat. Then she picked up the dog shampoo and lathered it over his long, matted fur. She could feel his ribs, but he wasn't underweight like most of the strays that were brought in.

'That's it,' she said, as she rinsed him. 'All done.'

The little dog tried to escape from the dog bath and scrambled out as soon as his ordeal was over.

'Lucky I have this towel,' Karen said, as she caught him in it and started rubbing him dry. Bathing him first meant the matted clumps were easier to cut away. By the time Karen had finished grooming him, Little Houdini looked like a completely different dog and a lot smaller.

'You must feel so much better now that matted fur is gone,' Karen said, looking at the smooth-coated dog. 'And you look a lot more handsome.'

Little Houdini whined. Karen took a small dog biscuit from a treat jar and offered it to him. The dog took it from her and crunched it up. But when Karen reached out a hand to stroke him he cowered away.

'Come and have a cuddle,' she said, patting her lap and holding her hands out to him.

All the dogs she'd ever known had liked cuddles. But not Little Houdini. He sat down close to her to eat the second biscuit she gave him, but not on her lap and not near enough for her to even give him a stroke.

'Poor little love,' Karen said. 'What did someone do to you to make you so scared?'

When he'd finished eating the second biscuit, she put a collar on him and clipped a lead to it.

'I'm sure someone will want you for a pet if no one comes forward to claim you,' she said, as she took him over to the kennels that were to be his new temporary home. She wished more people would come to the rescue centre and take a dog or a cat home with them. There were so many dogs and cats looking for a home and such lovely animals too. It was so unfair.

Little Houdini sniffed at the other dogs in their kennels as they passed them. The residents of the rescue centre ranged from pedigrees to cross-breeds, Great Danes to chihuahua crosses. Most had been given up due to family circumstances or the ill health of their owner. Some had to be removed because of cruelty or neglect. But a few, like Little Houdini, had been found wandering the streets.

The kennel Karen took him to had been hosed down, but it still smelt of the different dogs that had lived there before.

'In you go now.'

There was a fresh bowl of water in the corner and Bones had a long drink from it. Around him he could hear the other dogs, but he couldn't see them any more. He whimpered and lay down on the brown dog bed.

Chapter 3

The lesson before lunch was English.

'I want you to write down a wish,' Miss Dawson told the class.

Jake did his best to keep on lip-reading her when she stood up and started moving about.

'It could be a small wish, such as I wish it was fish and chips for dinner tonight, or it could be a big wish like I wish I was famous — only you'd have to think of what you'd like to be famous for. It could be a real wish or a wish that you make up, like I wish I could ride on a dinosaur or I wish I could fly. I want you to

write a paragraph in five minutes starting . . .'
She looked down at her watch. 'Now!'

Jake chewed on his pen. A wish. He only had
one at the moment.

'I wish I had a dog,' he wrote. But that wasn't
a paragraph so he carried on. 'It could be a big
dog or a little one. I don't care about that. It
can be any colour or breed or cross-breed.
Most of all I'd like a hearing dog, but if I can't
have one of those then any dog would do. I
want a dog to be my friend.'

'That's it. Time's up,' the teacher said after
five minutes. 'Now who wants to read their
wish out?' Most of the class put their hands up,
but Jake didn't. He never raised his hand if he
didn't have to.

'I wish I had more wishes,' said Chloe.
'There are so many things I want!'

'Good one.'

'I wish I could jump all the way to the moon
and back again,' said Moses.

'I wish I lived in a castle . . .' said Kiera.

'I wish I was a millionaire . . .' said Raj.

'I wish my dad would come back to live with us . . .' said Adam.

Jake looked down at the wish he'd scrawled across his piece of paper. His dad was often away for work – sometimes weeks at a time – but he always came home again. Jake missed him when he was gone.

'What was your wish, Tony?' the teacher asked.

'I wish I had a dog, miss,' Tony said.

But Jake didn't hear his answer and he'd stopped lip-reading to reread his own wish.

'I want everyone to expand their paragraph into a page now,' the teacher said, and Jake started to write about all the things he'd like to do with his dog, if he had one.

The lesson seemed to go much more quickly than usual and, when the bell rang for lunchtime, Jake followed the others out.

The school hall, which was also used for PE and assemblies, was exceptionally loud at lunchtimes. Jake found it just about impossible to hear anything as the voices melted into one another, creating one giant roaring sound.

He sat at a table with the rest of his class and pushed the food around on his plate. He didn't know that Tony had spoken to him until Tony touched his plate with his fork and then Jake looked up.

'This food's yuck,' Tony said, and Jake lip-read him and then grinned as Tony pretended to be sick.

'No messing about,' said the dinner lady.

Jake didn't hear the actual words, but he knew what she meant by her cross look. He looked down at his plate, still pushing his food around, and missed seeing Tony rolling his eyes.

As he took his plate back, he saw his little sister, Vicky, laughing with her friends. Vicky was in Year Three and everything was different for her. She didn't care how noisy the hall was. She could hear.

After school was over, Jake went along to the club for deaf and hard-of-hearing children that was held at the local youth centre. He enjoyed going there because they had a snooker table and a table-tennis table and video games. Sometimes they even went on trips to the seaside or the theatre. Jake liked it when they went to the signing pantomimes at Christmas. The rest of his family weren't as quick at signing as he was and so it took them all much longer to get any of the jokes. That made Jake laugh even more.

If a few of the children wanted to see a particular movie, the club would arrange a trip to the local cinema. Most cinemas had a loop system that they could tune into with their hearing aids.

Best of all, Jake liked going to the club because he could use sign language and the others there understood him and signed back. He also looked forward to it because Heather, who ran the club, had a hearing dog.

'I want one too,' Jake said, and he made the sign for dog, which looked like a dog moving two paws up and down and panting. He sat down beside her black Labrador, Bruno, and stroked his big old head. 'We've got a meeting at Helper Dogs tomorrow, but they told Mum there's a long waiting list,' he said, and Heather nodded as she lip-read him.

'Don't give up,' she signed.

Jake sighed and shrugged. He'd spoken more at the club in the few minutes that he'd been there than he had all day at school.

Before she'd started working with animals, Karen hadn't known how well they could tell the time. But she'd soon found out that it wasn't only humans who knew what should be happening and when. Animals did too, especially once a daily routine was established. The dogs at the centre all knew when it was feeding time and started barking and whining as Karen made her way round the kennels with the squeaky trolley, bringing bowls of food and fresh water for each dog.

When Karen gave Little Houdini his bowl of dried dog food, at first he just stared at it and then looked up at her.

'Go on then, Little Houdini,' Karen said. 'Eat up.'

All the other dogs had gobbled up their food as soon as she'd put the bowl down. But not Little Houdini.

Finally, he sniffed at it. The dried food didn't have the same delicious smells that he was used to and there wasn't so much as a single noodle in the tin bowl. He licked up a bit and crunched on it. Not bad. Not good either. But it was food and that was the main thing. He took another bite and then another as Karen watched and smiled from the other side of the bars.

'That's it.'

When the centre quietened down for the night, Bones looked at the bolt on the door of his kennel and the smaller hatch for putting food and water tins through. It was used for the more aggressive or very nervous dogs. The hatch was small, only a little bigger than a cat flap. But that didn't stop him from squeezing through it.

The other dogs watched from their kennels as the little dog trotted past them along the concrete floor to the exit.

Chapter 4

When Karen arrived the next morning, she found Little Houdini curled up on the comfy chair reserved for visitors. There was an empty packet of shortbread biscuits, also reserved for visitors, on the floor beside the chair and crumbs all over his furry face.

'I see you've made yourself at home,' Karen said.

He'd made it all the way to the exit, but wasn't able to escape because the door was locked.

Bones jumped off the chair, wagging his tail when he saw her. But when she reached out instinctively to stroke him he turned and jumped back up.

'Sorry,' Karen said. She hadn't meant to frighten him. 'Let's get you back to your kennel.' She clipped a lead to his collar and the two of them headed to the dog kennels, then Karen went to get all the dogs and cats their breakfast.

As she filled the different-sized food bowls, she couldn't help worrying about Little Houdini. How on earth was she going to be able to rehome a dog that didn't like to be stroked? Her only hope for him was Helper Dogs. They often trained rescue dogs as assistance dogs if they showed potential. Lenny said all dogs deserved a second, third and fourth chance. Maybe Helper Dogs could help Little Houdini get over his fear. She really hoped that they'd take him. Too many dogs were left unwanted and unclaimed.

'Are you looking for any special sort of dog today?' Karen asked Lenny, when he arrived at the rescue centre at a little after ten.

Lenny shook his head. 'Doesn't matter to me if it's big or small, pedigree or cross-breed. What I'm after is a dog that reacts to sounds. A dog that'll jump up and bark when the postman's still up the road from your house,' he told Karen in his soft Scottish burr. 'A dog that'll jump up when the phone rings or if it hears an unusual sound. Lots of pet dogs don't react, but some do and those make good hearing dogs because they're sound-sensitive.'

Karen thought Little Houdini might have all the makings of a hearing dog, but, as she explained to Lenny, she was still worried about him not wanting to be stroked. It was odd because he was such a friendly dog and obviously liked people. She found it quite heart-breaking when he backed away in fear because she knew he would be such a loving dog once he was sure he could trust a person.

Lenny tested three other rescue dogs before it was Little Houdini's turn. Roxy, the chihuahua cross, a collie called Peter and a Labrador named Nora. But none of them were suitable.

'Good dogs but not quite right to become hearing dogs,' Lenny said. It always made him sad when the dogs didn't pass the test. Especially if they'd been waiting for some time to be rehomed. But there was too much time and work involved in training a hearing dog to spend it on animals that were unlikely to succeed.

Karen took Lenny to Little Houdini's kennel.

'This little chap was brought in by the dog warden yesterday,' she told him. 'He isn't microchipped and has been living rough for some time. He's pretty streetwise and somehow ended up sleeping on the visitors' chair and eating our biscuits last night.'

Karen smiled at the memory and Lenny laughed.

'Sounds like he's got a lot of potential,' he said.

Little Houdini came over straightaway to sniff at the stranger and the bits of chicken and cheese in the dog-treat bag round Lenny's waist. He wagged his tail and then sat down and stared pointedly at the bag, his head tilted to one side.

'Can't be more than a couple of years old,' Lenny said.

He squeaked a toy that he had hidden in his hand to the left of Little Houdini and the dog immediately looked towards the sound.

'Good dog,' Lenny said softly, and he gave him a tiny bit of chicken from his treat bag.

Then he made a sound to the right and Little Houdini looked over in that direction instead.

Lenny smiled and made the sound one more time and this time Little Houdini put out his paw to the hand that Lenny had the toy in and looked him right in the eye.

'Very good,' Lenny laughed. 'Very good indeed! Let's see what he's like out of the kennel.'

Karen opened the door and clipped a lead to Little Houdini's collar.

As they walked together, Lenny was very pleased to see Little Houdini's interest in the different sounds around him. The little stray had lots of potential even if he did keep trying to choke himself on his lead.

'My major concern is his fear of being stroked,' Lenny told Karen. 'But he's got so much going for him otherwise that I'd really like to give him a chance. Maybe we'll try using an assessor hand and see how that goes.'

With dogs who were very nervous of being touched, they sometimes used a fake hand to stroke them, for a minute or so a day, and gradually built up the length of time before moving on to proper human–pet touch. By using the assessor hand, the dogs were able to sniff at it and no real scent came off it as it would a person's. But that could be a long, slow process.

'It's worth a try,' Karen said.

'How would you feel if I took him back to the centre with me and then home over the weekend to give him a proper assessment?' Lenny asked. 'I know he hasn't been here for seven days yet and someone may well come forward to claim him.'

Karen didn't think anyone was going to, but rules were rules.

'I'll microchip him now,' she said.

Lenny held Little Houdini while Karen injected him between the shoulder blades with the tiny chip.

'If you do get a call about him, I can bring him straight back, but I think he needs to be seen in a different environment,' Lenny said.

Karen looked down at Little Houdini and smiled. She was always pleased when the dogs got to be fostered in regular homes because she knew it was where they were happiest.

'OK,' she said. She'd never have let a stranger take a dog away for the weekend. But she knew Lenny and she desperately wanted Little Houdini to have every chance he could get.

'I'll let you know how he gets on,' Lenny said, as he led the little dog over to the Helper Dogs light blue van.

'You ready, Mum?' Jake called up the stairs. What was taking her so long? She'd spent ages eating her cereal and now she was spending ages putting on her make-up. He didn't want to be late. Dad had intended to come with them, but then he'd had to work. He was a long-haul lorry driver and sometimes, during the holidays, Jake got to travel with him.

'We don't want to be too early,' she said, coming down. 'Our appointment isn't until eleven thirty and it's only a short drive.'

'If we get there early, maybe they'll see us early,' Jake told her.

But his mum just shook her head as she picked up the car keys. That didn't seem very likely, but they could maybe see some of the dogs in training at the centre and she knew Jake would love that. She picked up the application form for a hearing helper dog they'd had to fill in and they went out to the car.

Jake sat hunched low in his seat. At least his mum had let him sit in the front for once. Usually Vicky was with them and his sister made such a fuss over whose turn it was to be in the front that it was easier for them both to sit in the back. But she wasn't there today because she'd had a sleepover last night and was spending the day at her friend's house.

Vicky was always being invited to parties or on fun day trips.

Jake sometimes took his hearing aids out when her friends came round because they were so noisy. He tried not to get jealous, but he never seemed to be asked to anything.

Today Vicky was going bowling with her friends and Jake was glad he wasn't. The last time they'd been, the server at the cafe there had given up trying to find out what he wanted to eat and had asked his mum instead. Jake had been so embarrassed. He wasn't a little kid. He could choose for himself. But the server hadn't given him enough time to decide and Jake couldn't hear what the 'specials' were.

The drive to the Helper Dogs centre took longer than usual because the old bridge over the river was being taken down that weekend.

'Lucky we left early,' Jake's mum said, as they finally turned into the driveway of the centre. 'Are you excited?'

'Yeah,' Jake said, but he said it quietly and his mum frowned as Jake looked out of the window. It wasn't that he didn't want to come here or that he didn't want a hearing dog of his own. He did want one badly, but he also knew that there weren't enough dogs that were suitable for deaf children to go around. His mum had told him he might have to wait for up to a year and he had a bigger worry that he hadn't told anyone. What if the dog didn't like him? What if it didn't want to be his dog? Maybe it would growl at him or turn and run the other way when he tried to say hello.

Jake sighed. He'd never get a hearing dog. Maybe there was no point even getting out of the car. But, just as he was thinking this, he saw a man opening the back of a light blue Helper Dogs van and a little smooth-coated tan dog jumped out.

Jake gasped as the dog looked right at him and wagged its tail.

Chapter 5

The next moment Jake had flung open his car door and was scrambling out.

'Jake . . .' his mum said, and she quickly jumped out of the car and headed after him.

Little Houdini backed away slightly from the boy running towards him and then looked up at him, his furry head tilted to one side, before taking two steps forward instead.

'What's his name?' Jake asked Lenny, as he reached Little Houdini and knelt down beside him. He didn't want to scare the dog so he made sure he wasn't too close and he didn't try to stroke him.

Little Houdini sniffed at Jake and took a step nearer. Sniffed again and came even closer until his fur was almost brushing against Jake's hand.

'Doesn't have a name yet. I've just brought him from the rescue centre. What do you think his name should be?' Lenny said, as he searched in the back of the van for Little Houdini's paperwork.

The dog sat down and looked up at Jake.

Jake frowned. What would be the perfect name for a hearing dog? Ears? That'd be a good one. Or maybe . . . maybe . . . yes, that'd be even better!

'Echo,' Jake said, and the little dog jumped up and started wagging his tail, as if he liked his new name. Jake reached out a hand and tentatively stroked him.

'Hello, Echo.' He kept on stroking him and grew more confident as he saw that the little dog liked it.

The newly named Echo stood up on his hind legs and put his paws on Jake's legs as the boy gave a soft laugh of delight.

Lenny finally found Echo's paperwork under his coat.

'He doesn't like to be . . .' Lenny started to say, as he turned round, and then did a double take when he saw Little Houdini being stroked and loving it. 'Echo it is then,' he said. 'I think he likes you!'

'Could he be my hearing dog?' Jake asked without thinking, but then he stopped and blushed. He knew he couldn't just have the first dog he saw. But it really felt like Echo should be his.

'Jake . . .' his mum said softly behind him. She'd already told him he might have to wait for a year or more.

'Got a lot of training to do before this dog is ready to be anyone's hearing dog,' Lenny said. 'And only if he passes all his tests.'

'Do most of the dogs pass?'

'About seventy per cent.'

'And what happens to those that don't?'

'We make sure we find excellent homes for them,' Lenny told him.

'If Echo doesn't pass,' Jake said, ignoring the look from his mum – he knew what it was like not to pass exams – 'could he be my dog then? It won't matter to me if he passes or not – I'd still want him.'

'Sorry for my son's bluntness,' Jake's mum said. 'He's not usually so pushy. Not ever really.'

'That's what meeting a dog can do,' Lenny said, as he watched Jake and Echo together. They certainly did seem to be getting along well. But it would be a while before they knew Echo's full potential. Although letting himself be stroked by the boy was a major, and unexpected, step forward.

Jake swallowed hard. He didn't usually like talking to strangers because he was worried that his words might sound wrong. But if he didn't say something now then he might not get another chance 'Can I help?' he said. 'Can I help with Echo's training? I'll work really hard and I won't get in the way and I'll do exactly what I'm told.'

'Echo's really got to you, hasn't he?' Lenny said, and Jake nodded as Echo gave his face a surprise lick.

'Yuck!' Jake said, laughing.

'And I can see the feeling's mutual. Well, we could always do with more volunteers,' Lenny grinned. 'You'll have to be committed though. It's no good turning up one day and not the next. Dogs don't understand that.'

'I'll be here,' Jake said. He wouldn't let Echo down.

Echo pushed his head under Jake's hand for another stroke.

'Jake, it's time for our appointment,' Jake's mum said, looking at her watch. She didn't want them to be late for the real reason they were here.

Jake hated to leave Echo. But if they didn't keep the appointment then he wouldn't be on the official waiting list for a hearing dog. His mum was already heading towards the reception.

'I'll see you later,' he told Echo, as he stood up.

Echo whined, but Jake had to go. The little dog watched as the boy ran off. He barked, but Jake had already gone inside the door to the Helper Dogs building.

'He'll be back,' Lenny told him, as he led him to his new kennel. But Echo only dropped down to the ground, with his head in his paws, looking utterly miserable once he was put inside. Lenny scratched his head. That boy had really made an impression on the little dog.

Inside the office, Jake and his mum sat on plastic chairs across from the assessor's desk. Jake's chair was closest to the window and he looked out of it.

'Now then . . .' the assessor, whose name was Lucy, said. 'As you know, hearing dogs are given to children with severe or profound hearing loss in both ears. Children who have trouble sleeping?'

Jake's mum nodded.

'Who are socially isolated?' Lucy said.

Jake's mum nodded again.

'Who suffer from low self-esteem?'

She looked over at Jake, but he was still gazing out of the window so his mum answered for him again with a nod.

Lucy reached over and touched Jake's arm. 'Jake, would you like a hearing dog?'

'I'd like Echo,' Jake told her.

After the assessment was over, Jake couldn't wait to get back to Echo and a dog-trainer apprentice called Becca took him to the kennel block.

When Echo saw Jake, he immediately jumped up and looked at him, his tail wagging fiercely. Jake ran over and put his fingers through the wire and Echo licked them.

'He really has taken a shine to you,' Lenny said, as he came back with a bowl of fresh water for the dog.

'He's brilliant,' Jake said. He'd wished for a dog and now it felt like his dream might come true.

'Come on now,' his mum said. 'Time to say goodbye.'

Jake really didn't want to go, but he couldn't stay here forever.

'Just a little while longer,' he said. Maybe he could take Echo for a walk.

But his mum shook her head. 'We need to pick Vicky up.'

Jake sighed. 'I'll be back soon,' he told Echo. But, as he started to walk away, Echo began to bark, as if he were telling him not to go. 'Actually, I'll walk home,' Jake told his mum.

'Are you sure?'

Jake almost never went for walks by himself because he was worried something might happen and he wouldn't hear it.

'Yes,' Jake said, and he raced back to Echo. The little dog ran round and round in circles and yapped excitedly.

'Where did he come from?' Jake asked Lenny, and Lenny explained that Echo was a stray who'd been picked up by the dog warden.

'He was only picked up yesterday so there's still a chance someone could claim him before the official seven days are up.'

'Official seven days – what are they?' Jake asked.

'It's the minimum amount of days until a dog that can't be identified can be rehomed,' Lenny told him.

Jake felt like he couldn't breathe. 'So Echo might belong to someone already,' he said. He should have known it was too good to be true.

Lenny saw Jake's stricken face and added quickly, 'We don't think so. He's been a stray for weeks and he isn't microchipped. The dog warden and rescue centre will contact the authorities, but it's very unlikely anyone will come forward.'

Jake nodded. But now he was worried. 'Six more days,' he said. Six more days until Echo couldn't be taken away.

'Why don't you take him for a walk?' Lenny said, handing Jake a lead.

'Can I?' Jake smiled.

'Yes, take him to the field over there, but don't let him off his lead. We don't want him running away.'

'OK.'

Echo walked on his lead much better with Jake than he'd done for Karen or Lenny. But he still tended to pull. Once they were on the grass, Jake stopped walking and ran with Echo instead. Echo wagged his tail as his legs raced along. This was much more like the speed he wanted to go.

When they got back, Lenny was waiting for them.

'I'm taking Echo home with me this afternoon and overnight,' he told Jake. 'To assess how he gets on in a home environment.'

'I wish he could come home with me,' Jake said.

'I know you do – you're a good lad and I can see he thinks the world of you. But for now can you help with his training here?'

Jake nodded and Lenny took Echo's lead from him. 'See you after school on Monday.'

'I'll be here,' Jake promised, giving Echo one last stroke. The little dog kept barking as he walked away.

The route from Helper Dogs to home was pretty straightforward and it was worth it because of the extra time he'd been able to spend with Echo.

Jake had walked for fifteen minutes and was more than halfway home when a hand touched him on the shoulder and scared him half to death.

'It's just me, just me,' said Tony, holding his hands up and stepping back when he saw that he'd made Jake jump. Anyone else would have heard him shouting and running up behind them. 'I live over there,' Tony said, pointing to a house with a white door. 'And I saw you from the window. Do you live near here?'

Jake shook his head.

'So how come . . .?'

'I've been to the Helper Dog centre. Been to see a dog,' Jake mumbled.

'A dog. That was my wish at school yesterday. Do you like dogs too?' Tony asked him.

Jake looked down at his feet and kicked at a pebble. 'It was my wish as well,' he said, looking back up at Tony.

Tony grinned at him. 'Excellent.'

'I want a hearing dog,' Jake said, feeling a bit more confident now. 'His name's Echo.'

'I just want a dog – any dog,' Tony said, as he headed back towards his house and Jake went with him. 'Come and see my room,' Tony said, when they reached the gate.

Jake hesitated for a second. Vicky was always being invited to other children's houses. But not him.

'This way,' Tony said, opening the gate and heading up the path.

Jake shrugged and followed him into his house and up the stairs, trying to act as if it were no big deal and the sort of thing he did every day. On the wall next to the stairs there were photos of Tony and an older girl, who looked a lot like him.

'Big sister?' Jake said.

'Yes, she's a pain,' Tony told him.

'So's my little sister,' Jake said. 'Right pain.'

'This is my room.'

Tony's room was full of posters of dogs, all sorts of different dogs, doing all sorts of different things.

'Mum says I can't have one because Tara's allergic,' Tony said, and he rolled his eyes.

'Sisters are so annoying,' Jake said, but at least Vicky wasn't allergic to dogs.

He looked at all the pictures of dogs, trying to find one similar to Echo, but there weren't any that looked exactly like the little dog he'd named.

'I'll take a photo of him on my phone next time I see him,' he told Tony, pulling his phone from his pocket and seeing that it had no power left.

'Hey, Jake,' Tony said, just as Jake was about to leave.

'Yeah?'

'Your dog might like this,' he said, and he threw Jake an orange-and-blue ball that Jake squeezed. It was soft in the centre.

'It squeaks when you do that,' Tony told him.

Jake grinned. 'Thanks!' he said.

'Where were you?' Jake's mum cried, when he finally got home. 'We've been worried sick. Helper Dogs said you'd left ages ago.'

'Mum was just about to phone the police,' Vicky told him. Her brother was so irresponsible.

'Been at Tony's,' Jake said.

'Who's Tony?' his mum wanted to know.

Jake thought for a moment and then he smiled. 'Friend from school,' he said. He liked saying the words – and having a friend.

Vicky and his mum stared after him as he headed up to his room.

'But he doesn't have any friends at school,' Vicky said.

Chapter 6

'Can I take him for a walk?' Jake asked, when he arrived at Helper Dogs on Monday afternoon.

Echo immediately jumped up and ran over to the kennel door, then looked back at Jake, as if to say: 'Come on then!'

'Do you think he understands the word "walk"?' Jake asked.

'Looks like it,' said Lenny.

'Most of the dogs know at least fifty words by the time they leave here, some of them maybe even a hundred. Echo's a very clever little dog,' Becca said.

Jake was really impressed. 'I bet most people couldn't understand a hundred different dog noises,' he said.

'We use signs as well as talking to the dogs because we know that whoever the dog is placed with will use one or the other of them, or both,' Lenny told him. 'But this one is most of the dogs' favourite sign.' He held both his thumbs up.

Echo's tail immediately started wagging and he came running over to Lenny and put his paw out.

'It means "good dog" and is usually accompanied by a treat,' Lenny said, as he pulled a little square of cheese from the treat bag on his waist and gave it to Echo.

Jake loved the idea that Echo would know sign language too.

'Can we go for that walk now?' he asked, and made the sign for 'walk' by wiggling his middle and index finger back and forth.

Echo jumped up as soon as Jake took his lead off the peg on the wall. Time to play!

Lenny watched the two of them heading off together. If ever a boy and a dog were made for each other, it was those two.

Jake pulled the squeaky ball Tony had given him from his pocket and threw it across the grass.

'Fetch!' Jake shouted, and he and Echo ran as fast as they could after the ball.

'Good dog,' Jake said, when they reached it. Echo picked it up in his mouth, looked up at Jake and wagged his tail.

Jake pulled a bit of chicken from the paper towel he'd wrapped it in at lunchtime when the dinner lady wasn't looking. Tony had given him a fish finger from his plate for Echo too and that was in another paper towel.

Jake threw the ball in the other direction and the two of them raced after it once again.

Echo thought the fish finger was just as delicious as the chicken.

'Sit,' Jake told him, and Echo tilted his head to one side. He'd heard the word 'sit' a lot today at the obedience class Lenny had taken him to.

'Sit,' Jake said, and then he made the sign for 'sit', which was a bit awkward as he really needed to use both hands. But Echo understood what he wanted and sat. 'Yes!' Jake shouted with happiness, as Echo jumped up, wagging his tail, and swallowed down the rest of the fish finger in one greedy gulp.

Jake took lots of photos of Echo on his phone and texted them to his dad who was travelling around Italy for work.

Sometimes in the school holidays he kept his dad company on his long-haul trips, sitting high up in the cab as they drove along the open roads. His dad would turn the radio up really,

really loud and they'd both sing along to it as loudly as they could. Vicky said Jake sounded like a strangled crow when he sang, but his dad didn't care.

He always made Jake laugh and Jake missed him when he wasn't there.

Piccola canaglia, his dad texted back a few minutes later, which apparently meant little rascal in Italian.

Echo was that all right. Jake sent him a thumbs-up emoticon.

He'd marked off the days until his dad was coming home on the calendar on the fridge. Until then his dad would have to make do with photos of Echo. He was sure his dad would love the little dog when he met him just as much as Jake did.

At school the next day Jake didn't go straight to his desk, looking down at his feet and avoiding everyone's eyes, like he usually did. Instead he went over to Tony and tapped him on the shoulder. He held up his phone so Tony could see the pictures of Echo he'd taken.

Tony especially liked the ones of Echo with the squeaky ball that he'd given Jake.

'He loved that!' Jake grinned.

He took his phone back as Miss Dawson came in and went to sit down at his desk at the front. He couldn't wait for the weekend when he'd be able to spend all day with Echo and not just a few hours after school. But he was also worried. What if his real owner came forward and claimed him? What if Echo was gone before then?

'How's it going?' Heather signed to Jake when he popped into the hearing club after school on his way to Helper Dogs.

Jake showed Heather a photo of Echo on his phone and Heather signed 'cute' and 'smart'.

Jake smiled. Echo was definitely both those things.

'Got to go,' he signed and headed off to see the little dog.

Chapter 7

It had been a whole week since Echo had been caught by the dog warden and brought to the dog rescue centre. A lot had changed for the little dog in that time, but no one had come forward to claim him.

Every morning he waited in his kennel for Jake to arrive and on Saturday morning Jake was there even before Echo had had his breakfast. Echo was so excited to see him he ran round and round in circles and then picked up a soft giraffe toy from his bed and brought it over to Jake.

'He's always very pleased to see you,' Lenny said. *And very sad when you go,* he thought, but he didn't say so because he didn't want to upset Jake.

The truth was Echo came alive when the boy was there and slumped when he left.

'The seven days are up,' Jake said, and Lenny knew immediately what he meant.

'Yes, and no one came forward so now we can train Echo to be a hearing helper dog.'

'So why did the person who had him before let him go?' Jake asked, shaking his head. 'And why didn't they report him missing? If he'd been my dog, I'd never have given him up, not even for a billion pounds, and I'd never stop looking for him if he was lost.'

'We don't know,' Lenny said. 'And Echo wasn't microchipped so there's no way to find out who his original owner was.'

No owner meant Echo could continue with his hearing helper dog training and hopefully one day become a hearing dog. Best of all would be if he became *Jake's* hearing dog. Only . . .

'What if he *does* belong to someone, but they didn't microchip him or it didn't work for some reason? What if there is someone out there looking for him?' Jake said. What if someone loved him just as much as he did and was searching for him?

But Lenny shook his head. 'Karen, who runs the dog rescue centre, contacted all the vets and dog wardens and lost dog sites, just as she always does for all the animals that are picked up on the streets. She circulated his picture to everyone she could think of, but no one knew of anyone looking for a dog matching his description.'

Jasper, the ginger-and-white cat, came over for a stroke.

'Jasper was another stray,' Lenny told Jake. 'He came here from the same rescue centre as

Echo. That was a few years ago now and he's made himself quite at home.' He stroked the cat who rubbed one side of his furry face and then the other side against Lenny's hand. 'He shows the helper dogs how cats prefer to be treated, don't you, Jasper?' The cat purred, as Lenny continued to stroke him.

'Echo seems to like him,' Jake said, as the little dog wagged his tail at the cat.

'Yes, and Jasper feels the same way. Sometimes he even tries to slip into Echo's kennel when I open the door. Echo's very friendly and the puppies here learn fast, but sometimes, for the rescue dogs who've been used to chasing cats, it's a lot harder to stop them from doing so.'

Once Echo had finished his breakfast, it was time for his training to properly begin. Jasper followed the three of them over to the training room, which was fitted out to look as much like a normal room in a house as possible.

Becca was there waiting for them.

'We need Echo to look at a person's face when his name's being called or signed,' Lenny told Jake. 'That's why the name Echo is so good and will help him learn to pay attention quickly.'

'Why?' Jake asked.

'Because of how it's signed,' Lenny said, and Jake's eyes widened and then he grinned as he did the sign: two index fingers going outwards from his chest and then one index finger coming back. Like it was returning or echoing.

'Echo!' Jake called, as he did the sign, and Echo immediately looked over at him and Jake held up his thumbs to let him know he'd done well.

'He's very good at making eye contact,' Lenny said. Some dogs needed a lot of practice before they actually looked someone in the eye.

'Better than me,' Jake agreed, and when Lenny looked over at him he looked down at his feet and then back up at him and grinned.

Jasper nimbly jumped up on to the made-up bed in the corner of the room, lay down on the pillow and went to sleep.

In the training room there was a doorbell on the back and front of the door, a phone on a small table, a smoke alarm on the wall, an alarm clock next to the bed that Jasper was now lying on and an oven timer beside an oven.

'It's harder for the dogs to learn what they need to do when the fire alarm goes off so we teach that last,' Becca told Jake. 'They have to know that they can't lead their owner back to the fire to show them what's wrong, but must lie down flat on the ground to clearly indicate that there's danger.'

'Let's see what Echo can learn,' said Lenny.

When the oven timer went off, Jake made the sign for 'Where?' with both hands at waist height, palms up and then moving them in a small circle as well as saying the word.

Echo looked up at him with his head tilted to one side and then looked over at where the sound was coming from.

'Good dog,' Jake said, as the two of them went over to the oven timer. He gave Echo a treat when they got there.

Becca rang the doorbell on the outside of the door to the training room and Echo looked over in that direction.

'Good dog,' Lenny said, and he gave Echo another treat.

Becca rang the doorbell again and Echo looked again and got another treat and lots of praise. Then the alarm clock went off and Echo looked over at that too.

'We're not expecting him to identify all the sounds yet and after a while we'll make them harder to find and move them around so they're not always in the same place. That'll come after he's learnt to alert you that there's a sound in the first place.'

Jake nodded as he listened to Lenny. There was no background noise of TV's or radios at the centre to distract him. Plus the room had a carpet on the floor and curtains at the windows. Soft furnishings absorbed sound and made it easier to hear with his hearing aids.

From what Lenny said there was a lot for the little dog to learn and it would take a great deal of concentration from him. Sometimes Jake got really tired at school when he had to concentrate hard to keep up with what was going on.

While Echo took a nap, Jake did his homework in the Helper Dogs cafe. His mum had made him promise that the dog training wouldn't distract him from his schoolwork. It was boring, but the thought of playing with Echo afterwards made him work harder than he ever had before and he was able to finish it quite quickly. Then it was back to the training room.

'We try to keep the training short and fun with lots of food treats. Always more positive than negative,' Lenny said. 'Because we want the dogs to be confident and to think for themselves.

'One of the first things I teach them is to fetch someone,' Lenny told Jake. 'The dog needs to alert a deaf person by touching them with their paw or nudging them with their nose. A bark won't do if someone can't hear it.'

Echo was lying beside Jake and didn't really want to go with Lenny when Lenny called him away.

'Go on, Echo,' Jake said, pointing at Lenny across the room, and finally Echo went, but he looked back at Jake all the time.

'Fetch Jake,' Lenny told Echo, as he pointed to Jake and Echo raced back to him, his tail wagging. Lenny shook his head. It wasn't quite what he wanted, but it was early days yet.

'Let's try to teach Echo to alert you by putting a paw on your leg. You sit over there, Jake; a paw on the leg is easier for Echo if you're sitting down. Now don't look at him.'

Jake sat down and turned away from Echo, as Lenny took the little dog by his lead and led him across to the other side of the room.

'Fetch Jake,' Lenny said. Echo raced back over, but Jake was facing away from him. Echo whined, but Jake didn't hear him. Echo tried to get round in front of Jake, but Jake moved so he was still facing away from him. Echo was now very confused. Finally, he jumped up at Jake to get his attention.

'Good dog!' Lenny cried. 'Good dog!' It was just what he wanted. 'Praise him, Jake.'

And Jake threw his arms round the little dog and told him how good he was and the next time Lenny sent Echo to fetch Jake, and Jake wasn't looking, Echo knew what to do. He put his paw on Jake's leg and, when Jake looked round, he wagged his tail and led him over to Lenny.

When Jake got home, he decided to have a go at making some home-made dog treats for Echo.

'What's that smell?' Vicky said, as she and Mum came into the kitchen. She had just come back from ice skating with her friends.

'Peanut-butter dog biscuits,' Jake said. 'I'm making some for Echo only there wasn't any peanut butter left so I used peanuts and a little bit of groundnut oil and blended them together.'

'We used to make home-made peanut butter when I was a girl,' Mum said. 'It's much tastier than from the shops.'

'They smell really good,' Vicky said.

'Taste good too,' Jake said.

'You've been eating dog biscuits?' Vicky said in horror. 'That's disgusting!'

Jake laughed. 'They're not so different from human biscuits. They don't have anything we don't eat in them only much less salt.'

Vicky tried one and nodded. 'Not bad at all,' she said.

Mum tried one too and gave a thumbs up as she chewed it.

'I just hope Echo likes them,' Jake smiled.

Chapter 8

On Sunday morning, Jake's mum gave him a lift to Helper Dogs and decided to come in with him.

'Just for a little while,' she said, when she saw Jake's less than enthusiastic expression.

Echo was, as always, over the moon to see Jake and he ran round and round in circles as Jake and his mum headed towards the kennels.

'Wish Echo'd make as much fuss when I turned up in the morning,' Becca said to Lenny.

'Jake's probably the first person Echo's loved or been loved by,' Lenny said, as Jake walked up to them with a big smile on his face. 'I'd say they were made for each other.'

'Me too,' Becca agreed.

Echo's training was a breeze when Jake was working with him, but a much harder slog when it was anyone else.

Echo stood on his back paws and wagged his tail and made excited, happy little whining sounds when Jake stopped outside his kennel.

'Morning,' Jake said, as Echo went just about crazy with joy. He gave the little dog one of the peanut-butter treats he'd made for him and as Echo gobbled it up he smiled. The little dog seemed to love them just as much as everyone else had.

Jake's mum watched him and Echo together. The little dog had changed her son from a boy who always seemed sad to one who usually had a smile on his face.

'Hello there, Echo,' she said, and, when Jake went to fetch a fresh bowl of water, she whispered 'thank you' to the little dog. Then she had a quick word with Lenny to thank him too.

'Here you are, Echo,' Jake said, coming back with the water.

'See you later, Jake,' his mum said. 'Bye, Echo, bye, Lenny.'

Jake gave Echo another of the peanut treats, which he gobbled down, and then he sat down and looked up at Jake with his head tilted to one side, his meaning crystal-clear.

'They're nearly all gone already,' Jake said, as he gave him another one.

He pulled the squeaky ball from his pocket and Echo immediately jumped up, his tail wagging, and looked over at the peg where his lead was hung.

'Ten minutes' play and then he needs to work,' Lenny said.

Jake grinned and grabbed the lead.

Echo tried his best to walk on a loose lead, but playing was so much fun and he couldn't wait to get to the field. Every now and again he forgot that he shouldn't pull and strained on his lead as he tried to get there faster.

At long last, they arrived. Jake unclipped his lead and threw the ball for Echo to race after. Echo picked it up in his mouth and came running back with it so it could be thrown again.

Jake was sure the little dog would be happy playing ball all day, but Lenny had said they only had ten minutes so after that they headed back.

'The next thing I want to teach Echo is how to deliver messages,' Lenny said, as he handed Jake a soft, waterproof, zip-up wallet.

Jake frowned at it. 'I don't understand.'

'If I wanted to give you a message to say "Come and watch TV" or "It's dinner time" or you wanted to send me a message like "Down in five minutes" or "What's for dinner?", Echo would be able to take the message to whoever you wanted and bring back their reply,' Lenny said.

'That's amazing,' Jake said. 'Can he really learn to do that?'

'Oh yes, and the rate he's going I don't think it'll be long before he's got it off pat,' Lenny said, as the three of them headed over to the training room where Becca was waiting.

The day whizzed past and, before Jake knew it, it was time to go home.

Tony was playing football outside his house, but when he saw Jake he came running over.

'How did it go with Echo?' he wanted to know.

The two boys walked on together, as Jake told him about all the things Echo was learning.

'He's so clever!'

In no time at all they were standing outside Jake's house.

'This is where I live,' Jake said.

'Oh,' said Tony. 'Well, see you at school then.'

As Tony started to head back, Jake called after him.

'You can come in if you like.'

And Tony grinned. 'Could do, for a bit,' he said.

'Oh great, you're home,' Jake's mum said, as he came in through the back door. 'I bet you're starving. How about some fish fingers?' Then she saw Tony behind Jake. 'Oh hello,' she said, looking surprised.

Tony nodded.

'This is my friend Tony,' Jake said. 'Want some fish fingers, Tony?'

'Um . . .'

'We've got lots,' Jake's mum said. 'You're very welcome to have some if you'd like.'

'OK then,' Tony said.

An hour later, Tony left as Ella's dad drove up with Vicky and her friends.

'Who was that just leaving?' Vicky wanted to know, as she came through the front door with Ella and Meera. They'd been to the cinema for Meera's birthday.

'Jake's friend Tony,' Mum said, and Jake grinned at Vicky's surprised face. It was nice to have a friend to eat fish fingers and talk about dogs with.

Chapter 9

The next Saturday morning Jake arrived at Helper Dogs only to find that he and Echo were going on a trip.

'The dogs in training need to have experienced all different sorts of transport,' Lenny said, as Jake stroked Echo. 'As well as going to places like hospitals, libraries, shops and cinemas, they need to be comfortable going anywhere their owner might take them.'

Echo looked over and wagged his tail at the new dog coming into the training centre.

'This is Pippa,' Becca said, as Echo sniffed at the twelve-year-old yellow Labrador and she sniffed back. 'She's a retired helper dog and she's coming along with us for the day.'

'Pippa will show Echo how he's supposed to behave at the train station,' Lenny told Jake while Becca went to get Echo's assessment form. 'It's often much quicker to have an experienced dog show an inexperienced dog what to do than have a person try to show them what's expected.'

Pippa lay down on the ground and Echo picked up his giraffe toy and dropped it next to her. Then the little dog sat down beside the older one.

'Although the dog's ability to sound the alert is our priority, the dogs in training must also pass this social aspect of their training before they can be qualified,' Lenny told Jake, as they watched the two dogs becoming friends. 'Helper Dogs needs to be sure that the dog will remain calm in all sorts of different situations. When we're training the puppies, we take them everywhere we can when they're as young as possible. But for the rescue dogs it can be a lot harder.'

'Why?' Jake asked, as Echo nudged Pippa with his nose and then lay down.

'Well, a little puppy will probably just accept going on a train as a normal thing to do – nothing to be scared of. But an older dog won't see it like that.'

'So how do they learn that there's nothing to be frightened of?' Jake asked.

'We do it by not being scared ourselves. By acting like we're not the least bit bothered, and the dog will take its cue from that. But you have to genuinely keep calm and not get all worked up, even if the dog is. Remember that they can feel if you're tense down their lead.'

'They can?' Jake hadn't thought of that.

'So keep Echo on a loose lead so he knows there's no reason to pull. Do you think you can manage all that?'

Jake nodded. 'Come on, Echo,' he said, as they headed out of the Helper Dogs kennels with Pippa, Becca and Lenny.

Echo trotted along beside Jake, looking up at him every now and again. But he was also very interested in all the smells along the way. Dogs who'd passed bushes and lamp posts, a cat hidden in a garden to the right, someone cooking curry to the left. The curry got a double sniff as it was a long time since Echo had tasted those delicious spices.

With his tail held high, the little dog skipped up the steps, and in through the train-station doors that slid open automatically, without any sign of fear at all.

'We should use the lift too,' Lenny said. Lots of dogs were worried about going in lifts. At least for the first few times.

Echo looked up at Jake and then back at the lift doors as they swished open.

Pippa went in with Becca, and Lenny pressed the button to hold the doors open as Jake and Echo followed them in.

'Good dog,' Jake said, and he gave Echo a treat as they went out on to the platform on the other side.

Echo gobbled the treat down and then looked up at Jake to see if there were any more. But, as the train roared along the platform, Echo cowered back and desperately tried to drag Jake into the lift. When Jake didn't move, he barked at him to tell him they had to get away, but Jake still didn't budge.

'Tell him it's OK,' said Lenny.

Echo whined because he knew it wasn't OK. Not OK at all. His little body shook with fear and he wanted to run, but he couldn't leave Jake. He looked over at the doors opening and slamming as people got on and off the train. And he tried to pull Jake away again.

'It's OK, Echo,' Jake said.

Pippa lay down on the platform as the train roared away and was soon no more than a distant speck. Time for a snooze.

'How come she's so calm?' Jake asked Becca.

Echo kept looking at where the train had disappeared to and then back at Jake. He pulled on his lead towards the lift.

'No, Echo,' said Jake.

'Pippa's been on lots of trains before because she used to be with someone who went to work in the city every day so she isn't at all fazed by them,' Becca said.

Echo whined and licked Pippa's face to try to wake her up when the next train raced along the platform without stopping.

This one was even faster than the one before. Echo was absolutely terrified as the great roaring beast came charging into the station. He barked at Jake to warn him and pulled on his lead and put his paws on his legs. Jake accidentally dropped the lead and suddenly Echo was free. He was desperate to get away from the noise of the train hurtling towards them. The wind drag from it tore at his fur as he dived under a bench further along the platform and the train raced on without stopping.

Lenny and Jake ran after the little dog.

'It's OK,' Jake said, crouching down and looking under the bench. He picked up the end of Echo's lead. Echo trembled with fear.

The train had gone and the station was quiet so when Jake took hold of his lead Echo crept out.

'There's nothing to be frightened of,' Jake told him.

Echo licked his hand, but his tiny body still shook. Jake hugged the little dog just as Lenny was about to tell him not to do so because it wouldn't help him get over his fear.

Lenny sighed. The transport part of the training was very important. It was one of the tests hearing helper dogs had to pass to become fully qualified.

Jake kept a firm hold on Echo's lead as the next train stopped on the platform and he lifted a trembling Echo up the steps because there was a gap between the platform and the train. Echo didn't mind the train once he was on it and they only went to the next stop.

'Here we are,' Lenny said, as the train pulled in to the station a few minutes later.

'What if he doesn't pass the test?' Jake said, looking down at his shoes.

'No point worrying about that yet. Sometimes dogs seem to think things through after the training's over for the day. I've often been surprised at them not being able to do something one day and then doing it perfectly the next!'

'Was it my fault?' Jake asked, swallowing hard.

'What?' Lenny asked.

'That Echo got scared. Was it because I was scared for him and he sensed it down the lead?' Jake said.

Lenny shook his head. 'No,' he said. 'Although him trying to protect you from what he saw as a dangerous, roaring beastie probably did make a difference. To his eyes it must've seemed like a landlocked Loch Ness monster was storming its way into the station.'

When Jake got home, he found Vicky in the kitchen stirring a bowl. 'What are you making?' he asked her.

'Treats for Echo,' she said. 'Cheese ones this time.'

'Thanks,' Jake said. He was really surprised that she was thinking of Echo. Maybe his little sister wasn't such a pain after all. At least not always.

'Why don't you try using this to cut them out?' Mum said, handing Vicky a small star cookie cutter.

'Brilliant!' Vicky said. 'Because Echo is a star.'

She gave Jake one to try once they were ready.

'Nice and crunchy,' he said, biting into the warm biscuit. 'Echo'll love them.'

Jake didn't tell his mum or Vicky, but he was really worried about Echo. If Echo didn't pass all of the tests, then Jake wouldn't be allowed to have him as his hearing dog. And that was just about the worst thing he could imagine.

Chapter 10

On Monday morning, Mum took a quick detour to Helper Dogs on the way to drop Jake and Vicky off at school.

Lenny had just arrived and was getting out of his van when Jake came running over.

'These are for Echo,' he said, handing him the bag of cheesy biscuit stars. 'My sister made them. They're to help him with his train test today.'

Jake wished he could go with Echo to the station again, but his mum wouldn't let him have the day off school and he wasn't sure that he would help by being there. Echo seemed to be as worried that the train would hurt Jake as he was worried that it would hurt him.

'Thank you,' Lenny said. 'We'll see you later and don't worry – we'll give him every chance we can.'

'I know.' Jake swallowed hard. It was impossible not to be anxious. There wasn't time to see Echo now, but he'd be back after school.

Everyone was heading in to class by the time they got to school and Vicky and Jake ran across the playground and went inside.

'Hope he likes my treats,' Vicky said.

'He will,' Jake grinned.

Jake couldn't think of anything besides Echo. All day long he worried about how the little dog was getting on. Was Pippa there to help him? Had he tried to run away from the train again? Lenny had said Echo would be allowed another two tries. If he still ran away after the third attempt, he would fail.

'Jake . . .' Miss Dawson said, and he looked up to find her standing right in front of him with a puzzled expression on her face.

'Yes, miss?'

'Everything all right?'

Jake blinked. Why was she asking him that? He nodded. 'Why?'

And then he looked around. Everyone else had already left the classroom for the day and he hadn't even noticed. He grabbed his school bag and hurried out after them.

A crowd of children had collected at the gates and as Jake walked towards them he saw Lenny. What was he doing at school? Then he realized that if Lenny was there then Echo probably was too and he started running.

Not only was Echo there, but Pippa and Becca were as well.

'What's his name?' the children asked Lenny.

'Why's he got that coat on?'

'Because he's a hearing dog in training,' Lenny told them. He was wondering if it was such a good idea to bring Echo to the school. The little dog didn't look happy.

As the children crowded round him and tried to stroke him, the little dog backed away from them and hid behind Lenny's legs. As Lenny had suspected, Echo was a one-boy dog.

'Echo!' gasped Jake, when he reached them, and Echo immediately came out from behind Lenny's legs, his tail wagging with delight.

'We thought we'd bring him to see you after the test as a special treat,' Lenny said.

'How did he get on?' Jake asked, as Echo nuzzled into him for a stroke.

'Not quite there yet,' Lenny said. 'But closer than he was.' And he smiled at Jake.

'Good.'

'He's in training,' Becca explained to the other children who wanted to pet Echo. 'It's best if you don't stroke him when he's working. You can stroke Pippa though.'

The truth was Echo wasn't the least bit interested in any of the other children. The little dog didn't even seem to notice anyone else now that Jake had come.

Vicky and her friends were watching. Jake looked so happy with the dog, happier than Vicky had ever seen him.

'Let's go and say hello to the dogs,' her friend Amanda said.

But Vicky shook her head. This was her brother's moment.

Chapter 11

Jake's dad came home unexpectedly on Friday evening just before the long weekend. Jake and Vicky told him all about what Echo had been up to.

'He's so amazing,' Jake said. 'You'll love him when you meet him, Dad.'

'He does sound pretty amazing,' his dad agreed.

'I made him some cheese dog treats,' Vicky told him. 'Echo really liked them.'

'Good for you,' Dad said. He was pleased that Vicky and Jake seemed to be getting on better. 'I can't wait to meet him.' Echo certainly did seem to be making a difference and Jake was so much happier.

'I haven't even met him properly yet,' Vicky grumbled. 'Although I've been to Helper Dogs, but only for a few seconds, and even then I had to wait in the car.'

'You will soon,' Mum said, but she didn't say any more after a look from Dad.

They had pizza for dinner and Dad told them all about his latest drive across Europe.

'We didn't think you were coming home for another week,' Jake said, and caught a glance between his mum and dad.

'Finished the job early,' his dad told him, as he took another pizza slice.

'When do you have to leave again?' Jake asked. He missed his dad a lot when he was away, even though he could call or text him whenever he wanted.

'Monday morning.'

'That's not long!' said Vicky.

'No, so we'd better make the most of it,' Dad said.

And Jake, who was always super alert, caught the half-wink his dad gave his mum. Something was definitely going on, but he had no idea what.

The next morning his dad came into his room, followed by his mum.

'This came in the post for you,' his dad said, and he dropped an envelope on Jake's bed.

'For me?' Jake said, as he picked it up. He didn't know who could be sending him a letter. But there wasn't one inside the envelope: it was an invitation.

Dear Jake and Family,

Helper Dogs is delighted to inform you that Echo has passed the final part of his hearing dog training test and will be receiving his coat on Saturday morning. We are pleased to invite you to a small award ceremony after which he will be allowed to accompany you home . . .

'He did it!' Jake shouted, as he punched his fist into the air. Echo was a hearing dog and not only that he was going to be Jake's hearing dog.

'What's happened?' Vicky said, coming into his room and jumping on the bed.

Jake showed her the invitation and she squealed. 'I can't believe we can bring him home!'

'But it's Saturday today . . .' he said, looking from his mum to his dad and back again. They were both smiling.

And then he realized what that look between them the night before had been about.

'You knew!' he said.

That was why his dad had finished his job early, so he could see Echo graduate.

'I didn't want to miss it, did I?' his dad said, and he ruffled Jake's hair.

'But what about the waiting list?' Jake said.

'Lenny said Helper Dogs' first priority is to their animals. You and Echo have such a special bond that he'd never be happy with anyone else,' his dad said.

Jake was grinning so hard that his face was aching.

'When they came to your school, Lenny said that it was clear Echo only really wanted to be with you,' Jake's mum told him.

'That's true,' Vicky said, remembering the other children crowding round Echo, but Echo only having eyes for her brother.

'Breakfast in ten minutes,' Jake's mum smiled, as Jake flopped back on the bed, clasping the invite to his chest.

This was the best day ever.

*

When Jake and his family arrived at the centre, they found Jasper in Echo's kennel but no Echo.

'Where is he?' Jake asked Becca.

'You'll see him at the ceremony,' Becca smiled.

Jasper came over to Vicky for a stroke and then the cat followed them as Becca led them over to one of the rooms in the Helper Dog centre where Lenny was waiting.

Vicky gave a squeal of delight when Jasper jumped up on to her lap and lay there, purring.

'We're here today to celebrate Echo passing the last of his tests to become a hearing dog,' Lenny said.

Echo came in with Becca, his tail wagging fiercely as soon as he saw Jake.

'Would you now take off Echo's hearing helper dog in training coat, Jake, and put his qualified hearing dog one on him instead?' Lenny said.

Jake stood up and Echo made happy little whimpering sounds, stepping from one front paw to the other as Jake came forward. Jake could feel his face burning. He didn't like everyone staring at him, but he kept telling himself no one was looking at him. It was Echo's big day and all eyes were on him.

Echo licked Jake's face as he knelt down and put the new coat on him. Everyone clapped and Echo looked up at Jake, knowing he'd done well, but not quite sure what it was that he'd done.

'Doesn't his tail ever stop wagging?' Jake's dad asked as he stroked the exuberant Echo.

'He certainly seems happy to be coming home with us,' Jake's mum said and Jake smiled.

There were forms for Jake's mum and dad to sign, but finally it was time to go.

'Echo loves going in cars!' Jake said, as the little dog happily jumped in the minute he'd opened the back door.

'That's because the trainers take the dogs on lots of short car journeys that have something fun at the end of them like a trip to the park,' Lenny said. 'Plus you're going in the car and wherever you are is exactly where Echo wants to be.'

Lenny showed Jake how to put on Echo's car harness so he'd be completely safe in the back seat. Jake's dad started up the car as Lenny waved them off.

On days like these, Lenny knew for sure that he had the best job in the world.

From the top of the Helper Dogs wall Jasper watched Echo drive away. Lenny went over to stroke him.

'We'll both miss him,' he said. 'But they'll be back to visit.'

Chapter 12

Once they were back at the house, Jake unclipped Echo's lead and Echo immediately made himself at home. He had no problem at all jumping up on to the sofa in the lounge, even though it was almost the equivalent of a person jumping their own height. He circled round twice and then lay down with his head on a cushion.

'Comfy?' Jake's mum asked the little dog when she found him.

Jake laughed because Echo certainly looked as if he were.

'He looks like he's lived here all his life!' Jake's dad said.

'That's because he's home,' Vicky said, and Jake smiled.

'Come on, Echo,' he said. 'Let's show you the garden.'

Echo immediately jumped off the sofa and followed Jake out of the lounge and through the kitchen. His little black nose sniffed at the interesting smells: bread in the bread bin, lots of nice things to eat in the fridge, the lingering smell of roast dinners coming from the oven.

Jake opened the back door and Echo wagged his tail as he trotted out into the garden. There were even more interesting smells here. A cat had been there recently, a hedgehog path ran round the edge and a family of mice lived under the shed.

Once Echo had done his business, they went upstairs.

'This is Mum and Dad's room,' Jake said, opening the door. 'And this is the bathroom.'

'This is my room,' Vicky said. 'And you're welcome in here any time, Echo.'

'Remember what we were told, Vicky,' Mum said. Lenny had made it clear that Echo needed to know he was there to help Jake. He was sure there was no need to worry in Jake and Echo's case, but sometimes dogs became confused when there were lots of people in a family fussing over them.

'Jake has to be the one who walks him, grooms him, pets him and gives him his food and treats, especially for the first few weeks.'

'It's not fair,' Vicky grumbled, as Jake led Echo to his room.

'And this is our room,' he told the little dog. He put his phone on his desk and then flopped down on to the bed. 'And this is our bed.' Jake patted the duvet and Echo immediately jumped up beside him and lay down.

A few moments later, Jake's mobile phone text alert sounded and Echo immediately sat up, looked over at where the sound was coming from and put his paw out to Jake.

'What is it?' Jake asked him, and he held his hands out in the sign for a question.

Echo led him over to the mobile phone on his desk and Jake smiled when he saw that he had a text message.

'Good dog,' he said, and he held up both thumbs. Echo was so pleased that he'd done well that he spun round and round in a happy circle.

The text message was from Tony. He'd put **Got** and then an emoticon picture of a dog and a question mark.

Jake took a selfie of Echo and himself. **Want to meet him?** he wrote and pressed Send.

Ten minutes later, the front doorbell rang. Everyone had been told not to open the door so that Echo would know it was his job to alert Jake.

Upstairs Echo heard the doorbell and whined and then put his paw on Jake's knee. He looked over at the bedroom door as the doorbell rang again.

'What is it?' Jake asked him and Echo led him down the stairs to the front door. He looked up at Jake and then at the door. When Jake opened it, he found a gasping Tony outside.

'Ran all the way,' he panted.

Echo wagged his tail and, as Tony crouched down to say hello, he put his paws on his shoulders and licked his face.

Mum and Dad and Vicky came out of the lounge where they'd all been waiting to say hello to Tony too.

'Come on up,' Jake said.

Echo raced up the stairs ahead of the two boys as if he were showing them the way. He ran straight into Jake's bedroom, picked up his ball in his mouth and started squeaking it.

'Echo loves that ball,' Jake told Tony, as Echo dropped it at his feet and looked up at him.

'Are you going to bring him into school?' Tony asked, rolling the ball across the floor for Echo, who pounced on it and then flipped on to his back, still holding it with his legs in the air, as the boys laughed. Echo jumped up, wagging his tail. He liked the sound of Jake's laughter very much.

'Maybe,' Jake said, and he gave Echo a stroke. 'If I'm allowed. I really want to.'

'Too right,' Tony said, as Echo picked up the ball and dropped it in front of Jake, who rolled it for him. 'And then he could play ball with us at breaktime.'

'He'd like that!' said Jake.

'See you again soon, Echo,' Tony said, when it was time to leave. Echo wagged his tail.

Later, when Jake's mum wanted him to come downstairs for his dinner, there was no point in calling because he couldn't hear her so she called Echo instead.

'Echo, Echo!'

Echo came racing down the stairs to see what she wanted, his tail wagging.

'Good dog,' Jake's mum said, and she gave him a small treat.

Then Jake's mum wrote 'Dinner time' on a Post-it note and put it in the soft, small wallet Lenny had given them.

'Call,' she said, pointing up the stairs. Echo ran back up and gave the wallet to Jake.

'Good dog,' said Jake, putting up his thumbs. He opened the wallet and took out the Post-it note along with a treat for Echo. Then he followed Echo down the stairs. It was time for the little dog's dinner too. Helper Dogs had given them some of the dog food they used as they didn't want Echo to get an upset tummy from a change of diet.

Echo crunched up the dry dog biscuits, but he kept looking over at Mum as she dished up the lasagne. Its cheesy smell was intoxicating.

Later, when they were watching the TV, Echo started pulling at the end of Jake's dad's trainer laces. He looked up in surprise at Jake as they came unravelled from the bow.

'Neat trick, *piccola canaglia*,' Jake's dad said, and Echo wagged his tail and then did the same thing with the other lace. 'I bet he could untie a rope too!'

Jake's dad pulled his trainers off and wiggled his toes inside his socks.

Echo started tugging at a sock. 'No, no, no,' Jake's dad said. 'I'll take my own socks off, thank you,' and he pulled off one sock and then the other, as Jake and Vicky laughed.

Usually Jake hated going to bed and would stay awake for as long as he possibly could. Often this meant he was so tired he almost fell asleep at school the next day. But it had been even worse when he was younger and the only way he got any sleep was if his mum and dad let him sleep in their bed with them.

Once he took his hearing aids out at night, he could hear almost nothing other than the tinnitus ringing in his ears. He wouldn't know if his mum or dad were calling him or if a burglar were in the house or if Vicky screamed. Knowing that was scary, especially when he was younger. It still frightened him now.

But tonight he didn't feel like that because he had Echo with him and Echo would let him know if there was anything wrong.

At bedtime he took Echo outside, filled up his water bowl, put it on a tray over by the window in his bedroom and climbed into bed.

'Come, Echo,' he said.

But before he'd finished saying the words Echo was already lying on the bed next to him.

Jake woke up in the night to find Echo on his back with his legs in the air. Jake rolled over and went back to sleep.

He woke again when he felt hot breath on his face, but he knew it was only Echo and he didn't mind a bit.

In the morning when he woke up he found Echo staring at him with his big brown eyes, already wide awake.

'Morning, Echo,' he said, and Echo pushed his head under his hand for a stroke and a tummy rub before jumping off the bed.

Time for breakfast.

Chapter 13

'Oh good, you're up,' Mum said, when Echo and Jake came downstairs.

Dad was drinking coffee, but Vicky wasn't up yet.

'We thought that as your dad's home for the weekend it'd be nice to go somewhere as a family for the day.'

'Where would you like to go?' Jake's dad asked.

Jake grinned. There was somewhere he really wanted Echo to see.

'The seaside,' he said.

'What about the seaside?' asked Vicky, rubbing at her eyes as she came into the kitchen.

'We're going there for the day,' Mum said.

'We are?' Vicky said excitedly. It was ages since they'd been there. 'Can Meera and Julie come too?'

'No, it's just our family today,' Mum told her.

'Better get your swimming costumes,' Dad said to Jake and Vicky. 'The weather forecast says it's going to be scorching.'

But Vicky was already racing back upstairs to find her bikini.

'You'll love the sea, Echo,' Jake said, as he grabbed his swimming trunks from a drawer and put them on under his jeans.

Echo wagged his tail. He didn't know what the seaside was, but he knew Jake was happy and that always made him happy too.

When they got back downstairs, Mum was pouring cornflakes into cereal bowls.

Jake measured out Echo's dog food in the measuring jug and put it in his bowl.

'Here you are, Echo,' he said, and they all watched as he gobbled it up before they crunched up their own cornflakes.

Jake loved watching the dog eat – especially when it was something extra tasty – because Echo's little tongue would go in and out as if he were really savouring it.

Echo sat next to Jake in the back of the car during the long two-hour drive. Some of the time he looked out of the window and some of the time he looked at Jake. Most of the time he slept.

'We're here,' Jake said at last, and Echo sat up and peered out of the window, catching the excitement in Jake's voice.

Jake unclipped him from his car harness, but kept hold of his lead. In front of Echo and as far as he could see to the left and the right lay yellow gritty stuff. He'd come across it sometimes on building sites. But he'd never seen this much of it in one place before.

He watched as Jake took off his trainers and then half pulled off one of his socks.

'Here, Echo,' he said, wiggling the end of his foot where the sock dangled. Echo grasped the sock in his teeth and tugged. Jake laughed.

As soon as Jake's shoes and socks were off, he wriggled out of his jeans and T-shirt and ran towards the sea.

'Come on, Echo!'

Echo went running with him. But as Jake ran into the waves Echo came to an abrupt halt at the shoreline and stared in horror. The water went on and on and the waves swept upward, rolled and crashed down. Echo shook with fear. Then, much worse, the waves crashed into Jake, and Echo ran back and forth along the water's edge, barking at Jake to tell him to come back out, to get away from the scary water. And finally he did.

'It's OK, Echo,' Jake said, as he flopped down beside him on the sand. 'No need to be scared.'

Echo licked Jake's face and wrinkled his nose. The boy didn't taste like he usually did. He was all salty.

Echo was very relieved when they headed away from the water back to Jake's mum who was lying on a rainbow-coloured towel and reading her book while Vicky and Dad went to get everyone an ice cream.

'Echo didn't go in the sea,' Jake said, and Echo looked up at the sound of disappointment in his voice, not sure what he'd done wrong.

'Well, he's probably not been to the seaside before,' Jake's mum said, pushing her sunglasses on to the top of her head. 'Give it another try in a little while.'

Echo might not have liked the sea, but he soon found out that digging in the soft sand was amazing. He dug and dug and dug and when Jake laughed it made him dig even more because he liked it when Jake made his happy noise.

He also liked the icy-cold, slippery-sweet taste of the vanilla ice-cream cone he was given and the fish and chips they had for lunch.

When the tide went out, it left little rock pools along the shore and these were much less scary for Echo than the sea. Jake lifted up a stone in a rock pool and a tiny crab came out. Echo put out a paw to try to stop it, but it was too quick and buried itself in the sand. He also tried to catch the darting shrimps and they were too fast as well but Echo liked paddling in the shallower pools and following Jake as he climbed over the rocks.

By the end of the day Echo was exhausted and slept all the way home. Jake felt his furry chest rising and falling and stayed as still as he could so he didn't wake the little dog.

'We should go out to celebrate,' Dad said, as they came back into town. Echo stirred and sat up and yawned.

Jake wasn't too sure. 'Why don't we just go home?'

But one of the things Jake's mum and dad were worried about was Jake's lack of confidence.

'Let's go and show Echo off,' Dad grinned.

Jake looked down at the little dog who gazed up at him with his head tilted to one side. He was wide awake after his long nap.

'OK,' Jake said reluctantly, and he put Echo's hearing helper dog coat on him.

Echo sniffed the air as they went into the Chinese restaurant.

'No dogs allowed!' the restaurant manager said, hurrying over to them with his hand outstretched, as if he intended to push them back out.

Jake turned to go. He knew they should have stayed home.

But his dad said: 'He's a hearing dog.'

The restaurant manager looked down at Echo's hearing helper dog coat. 'Oh sorry, I didn't see. Come in, come in. All assistance dogs *are* allowed.'

They sat out on the verandah and Echo looked up at the swaying paper-lantern chains and sniffed the air again.

One of the waiters brought Echo a bowl of water and when Echo saw him he stood up and wagged his tail.

'Does he know you?' Jake asked.

'I don't think so . . .' Li said. 'There used to be a dog that looked quite like him who came here for food. But he was just a stray and his coat was much longer . . .'

'Echo was a stray before he became my hearing dog,' Jake said.

Echo sat down and looked pointedly at Li and then put out his paw to him.

'One moment,' Li said, and he hurried off, then came back holding his phone in one hand and a bowl of chicken fried noodles in the other. 'They're not hot – may I?' he asked, pointing to Echo, who was now standing up and drooling at the sight of one of his favourite meals.

His face was in the noodles and slurping them up almost before Li had put the bowl down on the ground. On his phone Li found the photo of the stray dog, also eating noodles, that he'd taken a few months ago.

'Look!' he said, as he showed it to Jake and his family.

The dog in the picture certainly looked a lot like Echo, especially now Echo had noodles hanging from his mouth too.

Li went to find more staff who'd met Echo previously when he was a stray and soon there was a crowd of people around the table on the verandah until finally the restaurant manager told them all to go back to work.

'You're welcome any time,' Li said, after Jake and his family had finished their meal. He looked over at his dad, the restaurant manager, and his dad nodded. 'Plus free noodles for the dog!'

'Echo loves noodles,' Vicky laughed.

'Well, that wasn't so bad, was it?' Jake's mum said, squeezing his hand as they left the restaurant.

'It was amazing,' Jake grinned. The whole day had been amazing. He looked down at the little dog beside him. Everything was a hundred, no a thousand, times better now that Echo was here.

Chapter 14

One of the many things that Echo had experienced as part of his hearing helper dog training was going to the supermarket. But Jake still didn't really want to go there. He'd refused to ever since the lady had called him a 'rude boy' and pushed her trolley into him.

'It wasn't you who was rude, it was her,' his mum said.

But that didn't make him feel any better or want to go to the supermarket again.

'What if she's there?' he said.

'She won't be.'

Jake soon found out that a trip to the supermarket with Echo in his hearing helper dog coat was completely different. Usually no one spoke to him, but they did now.

'What's his name?' the other customers asked Jake.

'What a poppet!' they said, as Echo wagged his tail.

'A hearing dog – I've never met one of those before.'

Echo had stopped in the dog-treat aisle and was staring at the gravy-bones boxes on the bottom shelf. Jake was just about to pick up a packet for him when Echo took the initiative and nudged one off the shelf and on to the floor.

'OK, OK,' Jake said, picking it up. 'You can have it.'

He dropped the box of gravy bones in the trolley when they caught up with his mum.

'Echo wants these,' he said, and his mum smiled.

After they'd been to the supermarket, his mum dropped Jake and Echo off at the club for deaf and hearing-impaired children.

Jake liked going there because there wasn't as much pressure as there was at school. Everyone there understood each other and they used a mixture of speech and lip-reading and signing. As soon as he walked through the door, he always felt like he could stop holding his breath.

'See you later,' Mum said, as Echo and Jake got out of the car. 'Do you want me to pick you up?'

'No, we'll walk,' Jake said. He loved walking with the little dog and he knew Echo would alert him if need be.

Heather's hearing dog, Bruno, was much older than Echo, almost thirteen. Mostly he liked to lie on his soft padded mat and snooze, but he flapped his tail up and down and staggered to his feet to say hello to Echo when

Jake and the little dog came in. Heather had been offered a new hearing helper dog, as Bruno was getting too old to do all he needed to, and was getting a little bit deaf himself, but Heather didn't want a new dog and so she and Bruno managed as best they could together.

'Just having him around makes all the difference,' Heather said.

Jake smiled as he stroked both dogs at the same time. He knew exactly what she meant. He'd only had Echo for a few days, but his whole world had been transformed. He was smiling all the time now. Echo wasn't only his hearing dog – he was his furry best friend too.

'A thousand times better,' he signed and Heather nodded.

All the other children at the club made a huge fuss of Echo and Echo's little tail wagged non-stop. The morning whizzed past and, before Jake knew it, it was after twelve. Time to head home.

But when they got outside it was pouring with rain and Echo whimpered as he cringed away from it. There was a bus stop just outside and a bus heading towards it. The bus route went past Jake's house, but he'd never been on one by himself. He didn't like going on buses, or any public transport, alone because he couldn't always hear what the bus driver said. But Echo really hated the rain. His hearing helper dog coat was already soaked through and Jake didn't want him to catch a cold. So he held out his arm and the bus pulled up.

'One for me and one for my dog,' he said.

The ginger-bearded driver looked at Echo's hearing helper dog coat and then back at Jake. Sometimes beards made it much harder to lip-read a person because the beard covered their lips. But the bus driver's beard wasn't too bad.

'Hearing dogs travel for free,' he said, and Jake and Echo carried on down the bus to take a seat.

Jake picked Echo up and let him sit on his lap for the short journey home. Everything was so much better with Echo. Things Jake would have avoided doing, like getting on the bus and worrying he wouldn't understand the driver, didn't seem such a big deal when he needed Echo to stay dry. He buried his face in Echo's wet fur.

'He's a good little dog,' the woman who came to sit next to Jake said, but Jake didn't hear her so she touched his arm and when he looked up she said it again.

'Yes, he is,' Jake agreed. 'His name's Echo and he's super smart too.'

'How did it go?' his mum asked him, as she made him a sandwich when they got home.

'Brilliant!' Jake told her. 'We went on a bus.'

'*Re-ally?*'

Jake grinned at his mum's surprised face. He felt like there was nothing he couldn't do with Echo beside him.

Echo looked pointedly at Jake's cheese and ketchup sandwich. But Lenny had warned them not to overfeed him.

'He's only a little dog and his eyes are bigger than his belly,' he'd said.

But Jake didn't want Echo to be hungry so he gave him a few gravy bones instead.

From upstairs came a shriek and the thump of someone jumping off a bed.

'Vicky and her friends are doing karaoke,' said Mum.

Jake rolled his eyes as the music was turned up and pounded out from above.

When the gravy bones were gone, he and Echo headed up the stairs to Jake's bedroom and closed the door, but it was still noisy and he wanted to do his homework so he took his hearing aids out. That was much better, although he could still feel the vibrations of the music through the floor.

Echo hopped up on to the bed, not bothered by the sound of the music at all, and Jake went to join him. Jake did his homework while Echo fell asleep beside him. It had been a long morning for the *piccolo canaglia*.

Without his hearing aids, Jake couldn't hear when Vicky called Echo. But he knew she must have done when Echo jumped off the bed, put one paw on Jake's leg and looked towards the bedroom door.

'I want Echo to come with me,' Vicky said, when he opened it. 'Why does he always have to be with you even when he's not on duty? It's like the two of you are superglued together.'

'He can go where he likes,' Jake told her, but secretly he didn't want Echo to spend too much time with Vicky. It was nice that they both loved Echo, but she had lots of other friends.

Jake held his breath as he lip-read Vicky's words. 'Come on, Echo . . . *tre-ats*!'

Jake looked at Echo. How was any dog supposed to resist the word 'treats'? But somehow Echo did. He gave an involuntary whine that Jake didn't hear before hopping back on to the bed and resting his chin on his paws.

'Good dog,' Jake said, joining Echo on the bed and giving him a stroke as Vicky stomped off to her room and the karaoke music started again.

Chapter 15

Jake opened his eyes and smiled at the feel of a lick on his face.

'Morning, Echo,' he said sleepily, and Echo rolled over on to his back so Jake could give him a tummy rub.

Today Echo was coming to school with him so everyone there could meet him for the first time.

'He probably won't be allowed to come in with you every day,' Jake's mum warned him, as she dropped Jake and Vicky off at the gate. She was going to bring Echo to the school once all the children had gone inside.

But Jake secretly hoped that once the Headmaster had met Echo he'd say he could be there every day, especially if Jake promised that the dog would be no trouble at all.

Echo tried to get out of the car with Jake.

'No, Echo, you wait,' Jake said, as Vicky ran off to join her friends.

'Otherwise everyone will want to stroke him at once and it'll be too much for him. It'd be too much for any dog,' Jake's mum said.

Echo whined and put out his paw to Jake.

'I'll see you soon,' Jake told him.

But that wasn't enough for Echo. He barked at Jake not to forget him and then he barked some more and put his paws up on the car window – his eyes never leaving Jake as he walked away.

'It's OK,' Jake's mum said. 'Hush now.' But Echo wouldn't be distracted.

Tony was waiting for Jake at the gate. 'How's Echo?' he said.

'You'll be able to see for yourself in a minute.' Jake grinned, as he explained that Echo was going to come into school for the day.

'Brilliant!' Tony said, and they walked into the classroom together.

'He's different,' Chloe said, when Tony and Jake had been in the classroom for a few minutes, laughing about Echo and the Chinese noodles.

'Course he's different,' Tony told her. 'He's got a dog now.'

But Chloe shook her head. 'It's not just that – he even looks different,' she said.

'I am standing right here!' Jake told her.

'You wouldn't have said that for a start,' Chloe said, only now she was talking directly to him and looking him in the eye. 'It's like you've grown five centimetres and you don't look down at the ground any more. Your shoulders used to be all hunched up, but now your head's high.'

After Miss Dawson had taken the register, they all headed to the hall for a special assembly. Miss Dawson stood at the front and when all the classes had arrived she told them a hearing dog was going to be visiting them.

'His name's Echo and you'll know who he is because he'll be wearing his light blue hearing helper dog coat. Plus he should be the only dog here,' she joked. Miss Dawson loved making jokes. 'He's going to be with Jake in my class. Wave your hand, Jake, so everyone can see you.'

Jake waved his hand but not very high.

'Higher, please,' Miss Dawson said.

Jake raised it a bit and waved again.

'Echo is Jake's hearing dog,' Miss Dawson told everyone. 'So if you see him and Echo about today don't forget to say hello.'

*

When Jake didn't come back to the car, Echo whimpered.

'Look, Echo. What's this?' Jake's mum said, waggling a chew in front of him. But Echo wasn't interested in chews today. He stood on his back legs with his paws on the window, willing Jake to return.

Fifteen minutes later, Jake's mum looked at her watch. It was time to take Echo into school. She opened her door and was going to get Echo out of the other side, but he nimbly jumped on to her lap and was almost out of the car before her. She only just had time to grab hold of his lead.

'It's lucky you're a little dog,' she said, as Echo dragged her in the direction Jake had gone, straining at the lead. Echo pulled her through the gate and into the playground. But there he lost Jake's scent and looked up at Jake's mum pitifully and whined.

'Don't worry, I know where he is,' she told him, and then felt a bit embarrassed talking to a dog who couldn't understand her. She was glad no one had seen her. She pulled open the swing doors and they went into the school.

'Oh, isn't he sweet?' the receptionist said, coming out of the office. 'I love dogs.'

She reached down to stroke him, but Echo backed away and pulled Jake's mum further down the corridor. He wanted to find Jake.

'Sorry,' Jake's mum said over her shoulder, as she was dragged along behind him. He was very determined and surprisingly strong for a small dog.

Echo sniffed at the floor and didn't pay any attention to the people they passed – not the caretaker or the girl whose mum was taking her to the dentist. He was surrounded by the smell of lots of children, but every now and again there was a very faint scent that made his tail wag hard and his heart beat faster. He could smell Jake was close by.

He dragged Jake's mum into the art room where Jake had a picture on the wall. But the room was empty now and Echo whined.

'This way, Echo,' Jake's mum said, and they headed on down the corridor.

Echo's nose caught the scent of the rat family that lived under the lockers, and the caretaker's cat who sometimes came in with him at the weekends.

As they passed the kitchens, there was the delicious smell of school dinners cooking and Echo's tail gave an involuntary wag. And then suddenly the scent of Jake filled his nostrils and he knew he was close, very close, and his tail started wagging very hard.

Jake's mum pushed open a classroom door and thirty children looked round. But Echo was only interested in one of them. The little dog's tail wagged and wagged as Jake walked over to him.

He made happy, excited little noises and hopped from one paw to the other as Jake knelt down beside him and pressed his face into his fur. Then Echo licked his face over and over.

'Yuck! That's disgusting,' Chloe said.

'Not if you're a dog,' Tony told her.

Jake took Echo's lead from his mum and led him over to his desk and sat down. His desk no longer felt lonely now that Echo was here.

Miss Dawson made sure all the children stayed in their seats while Echo got used to being in the classroom.

'Just pretend Echo isn't here,' she told them.

But of course that was just about impossible to do so Miss Dawson gave them a spelling test to make them all concentrate.

Jake chewed on the end of the pen as he tried to work out the answers. Echo whined but when he saw Jake was busy, and Jake whispered the words 'work time', he lay down under the desk instead.

An hour later, Echo heard the bell ring. Immediately he jumped up and put his paws on Jake's leg, but then he lay down flat on his tummy just as he'd been taught to do.

'It's OK,' Jake whispered, not sure why Echo was acting this way. No one else seemed to be reacting as if there was anything wrong. He stroked Echo's furry head as Miss Dawson finished what she was saying and told the children they could go outside for breaktime once everyone else had come in.

'I don't want Echo being swamped by children on his first day here,' she said.

So they waited until the second bell rang and all the other children came back inside. Once again, Echo touched Jake's leg with his paw when he heard the bell and then lay down. Once again, Jake told him there was nothing wrong. Echo whined.

'Now you can all go outside,' Miss Dawson said.

Jake clipped Echo's lead to his collar as everyone stampeded for the door.

'Don't run! Be careful!' Miss Dawson called after them.

Echo watched Jake take his squeaky ball from his school bag and put it in his pocket. His tail wagged very fast as he looked up at him. It was time to play and he loved playing! Jake took off Echo's hearing helper dog coat so he'd know he wasn't on duty.

There were lots of children to avoid as Echo ran after his squeaky ball that Jake and Tony threw for him. Plus it was much bouncier than when they usually played on the grass.

Echo dived under a wooden bench to retrieve it from behind the dustbins that smelt of interesting things to eat.

When the bell rang for the end of breaktime, Jake didn't hear it but Echo did. He ran over to Jake and nudged his hand and then lay down flat on the floor.

'What's he doing?' Tony asked him.

'He's letting me know there's the sound of an alarm,' Jake said, biting at his bottom lip. 'But I don't know why he's doing it.'

'That's what the lesson bell sounds like,' Tony told him. 'They use the fire alarm.'

'They do?' Jake sighed with relief. 'Good dog, Echo,' he said.

Echo stood up and wagged his tail as they went back indoors and headed for their seats.

Chapter 16

'This term we're going to start a new topic in honour of our very special visitor, Echo,' Miss Dawson said, when Jake had put Echo's hearing helper dog coat back on him and everyone had sat down.

When Echo heard his name, his tail flapped up and down and he looked up at Jake, but he didn't get up because Jake was still looking at the front as he lip-read the words Miss Dawson was saying.

'It's going to be about dogs. Who thinks they know when we first had pet dogs?'

'Fred Flintstone's got a dog – I'd say Stone Age,' said Tony.

'He doesn't have a dog!' Chloe said. 'He's got a dinosaur called Dino that acts like a dog and everyone knows dinosaurs and people didn't live at the same time in history.'

Tony poked his tongue out at her, but Chloe just laughed. 'They'd have had *wolves* not dogs,' she said.

Miss Dawson nodded. 'Did you know that a little dog called Robot found over six hundred cave paintings in a cave in France?'

'What?'

'How?'

But Miss Dawson wouldn't tell them. 'Maybe one of you would like to find out for your project,' she said.

'I want to do my project on Robot,' said Sahi.

'Are all dogs really wolves, miss?' asked Ben.

'Another good question that could also be a project,' Miss Dawson said. 'Are pet dogs related to wolves or did they evolve from wolves? But then again are foxes a type of dog and what about hyenas?'

'And jackals and coyotes, miss. Don't forget them.'

'Precisely. But your project doesn't have to be about the history or genesis of dogs. It can be anything at all to do with dogs.'

'I want to do one on dog fashion,' Amos said.

'Good idea.'

'I'm going to do it on royal dogs . . .'

'Parachuting dogs . . .'

'Surfing dogs . . .'

'Dog film stars . . .'

'Police dogs . . .'

'Do we have to write lots?' Amos asked. 'I'd rather make things than write about them, miss.'

'It doesn't matter as long as you work hard at it. I want everyone to give a short presentation on their chosen topic at the end of term.'

Jake gulped. More than anything he hated getting up in front of other people, but he did like the idea of doing a project on dogs and the time until the lunch bell rang went very quickly.

This time when Echo heard it and lay down flat on his tummy Jake knew the reason why.

'Good boy, Echo.'

Tony came to join him as he and Echo headed into the lunch hall. Jake wanted to get Echo some water, but he was too embarrassed to ask the dinner ladies.

'I'll ask for you,' Tony said, and a few moments later he returned with an empty plastic bowl full of water. He put it close to Echo who had a long drink. He'd only just finished when one of the dinner ladies came over.

'I wondered if your dog would like some chicken?' she said to Jake, and when Jake said he would she brought a small paper plate full of meat over to Jake's table.

Echo wagged his tail and let the dinner lady stroke his head before his head went down and the chicken was gobbled up.

'I think he liked that,' she laughed and Jake nodded. Maybe the dinner ladies weren't so scary after all.

Jake's mum texted him.

How's it going?

Best school day ever! Jake texted back.

Do you want me to come and pick Echo up?

No way!

They did more on the dog project after lunch.

'So it can be absolutely anything at all about dogs?' Chloe asked Miss Dawson.

'Yes, and there's lots of interesting topics to choose from. Did you know that Florence Nightingale's first patient was a sheepdog called Cap?'

'No – what happened?'

But Miss Dawson only smiled and shook her head.

'You can look it up when we go to the computer lab,' she told her class. She looked at her watch: still fifteen minutes before they could go there.

'Find a partner and have a *quiet* chat among yourselves about your ideas,' she told the children.

Jake looked down at his desk. No one ever wanted to be his partner.

Around him children moved chairs and swapped seats so they could be next to each other. The room was full of excited voices discussing different projects.

Jake felt the empty chair beside him being pulled back and when he looked up he saw Tony grinning at him.

'Partners?' Tony said.

'Partners,' Jake agreed and beamed back at Tony, as Echo stood up and wagged his tail.

'I'm doing mine on search-and-rescue dogs,' Tony said.

'I'm doing mine on hearing dogs and Echo,' Jake whispered. Or at least he tried to whisper, but one of the things his hearing loss meant was that he couldn't tell how loudly he'd spoken and when everyone turned round to look at him he realized they'd all heard. But Miss Dawson didn't mind.

'Good idea, Jake,' she said.

In the computer lab Tony took a seat next to Jake, and Echo sat under the table. Jake looked at the Helper Dogs website. He clicked on the History of Helper Dogs button.

'Helper Dogs was started with just two dogs twenty years ago. The first fully qualified hearing helper dog was called Mitsie. She was a bit of a character and loved eating fruit and vegetables. Her favourite fruits were tangerines, which she was able to peel for herself.'

Jake frowned. He wasn't sure how she peeled them. With her claws? Or with her teeth? It didn't say.

There was also a picture of Mitsie. She was a Jack Russell cross and she looked cheeky and mischievous, just like Echo. Jake thought she and Echo would probably have been friends, although as far as he knew Echo didn't like eating tangerines.

At least for his presentation at the end of term he already had some props, like Echo's coat and collar and his squeaky ball.

Echo nudged his hand with his head and Jake stroked him and then said, 'Work time,' and Echo lay down and went back to sleep.

'I'm doing my project on Rip,' said Tony.

Jake didn't hear him so Tony touched his arm and repeated what he'd said. But Jake only managed to lip-read the last word.

'Trip? Who tripped?' he said, looking around.

Tony grinned and shook his head. 'Not trip – Rip!' He pointed at the picture of the little dog on the computer screen who'd won a Dickin Medal for his search-and-rescue work in World War Two.

'Good one,' said Jake.

'So what makes it easier for you to hear me?' Tony asked, and Jake frowned as he thought.

'When you look at me when you're talking,' he said. 'Look me in the eye and keep facing me.'

'I do that already,' Tony said confidently, but Jake shook his head because that wasn't always true.

'What about when you look at the computer screen at the same time you're talking to me?'

Tony looked at him and then back at the computer. 'Must make it a bit tough?' he asked.

'Very tough.'

'OK, what else?'

'It's hard when there's lots of background noise or when it's dark. You try lip-reading in the dark!'

Tony laughed.

'And don't give up,' Jake said. That was the worst thing. Sometimes people just stopped trying to talk to him if he didn't understand straightaway.

'I won't,' Tony promised.

'Try explaining it a different way if I don't get what you're saying, or even write it down. But don't give up. Don't think it's not worth bothering. Don't think it doesn't matter because it does. I want to know what's going on. I don't want to be left out.'

'OK, OK,' Tony said, but he looked in Jake's eyes when he said it.

'Right,' grinned Jake. He'd talked far more than he usually did.

'We should get the rest of the class to try it.'

'Try what?'

'Try being deaf and see if they can lip-read. Learn a few signs. See what it's like.'

Miss Dawson overheard the two boys and thought that sounded like a very good way to spend the rest of the afternoon once they went back to class.

First she got Jake to show them how he signed Echo's name.

'Both index fingers come out from your chest and then one index finger returns,' Jake said. 'And you say the word "Echo" at the same time.'

Echo looked around at the children and then up at Jake. He wasn't sure why everyone was signing his name, but Jake was smiling at him so he must have done something good. He wagged his tail.

'How would you do my name?' Tony asked, and Jake showed him how to sign the letter 'T' by using his hands. Tony copied him.

'If it's someone's name, you don't always need to finger-spell it all – just the first letter will do,' Jake said.

'What about mine?' Chloe said, and Jake cupped his hand to form a C and Chloe copied him.

Everyone wanted to know how to sign their own name and Jake finger-spelt most of the alphabet with them.

Because sign language was something he knew lots about, he didn't feel too embarrassed standing at the front. Plus he had Echo there, and with the little dog beside him he didn't feel as self-conscious as usual. Although he was still pleased when it was over and he could go and sit down.

'Thank you very much, Jake,' Miss Dawson said, smiling. 'That was really interesting. Now how do I sign "home time"?'

Jake grinned and put the fingers of both

hands together like a roof and touched his watch. Miss Dawson copied him.

'See you all tomorrow,' she said, as the bell rang.

Echo touched Jake's leg and lay down on his tummy. Then he jumped up and wagged his tail as the children stood up and he and Jake followed them out of the classroom.

Chapter 17

On the way home from school Jake and Tony took a shortcut through the park. But today it wasn't almost empty as it had been the last time Jake and Echo had been there. Stalls were being set up and caravans were parked on the grass.

A man in a brown suit was looking at a clipboard and directing the stallholders to where they should be.

'What's going on?' Jake said, as Echo sniffed at the smell of hot dogs and burgers, pakoras and onion bhajis cooking.

'They're setting up for the Fresh Start Festival at the weekend,' Tony told him. 'There're going to be over a hundred stalls, plus bands playing and dancers and re-enactors and fire-eaters.' He was looking forward to seeing the fire-eaters. 'My sister Tara's helping on the face-painting stall. All the money that's raised is going to help fund the Fresh Start Hostel next to the park. By tomorrow this place'll be full of stalls.'

And noise, thought Jake. It was much easier for him to hear when there wasn't a lot of background hubbub. The festival didn't sound like fun to him, even if it was for a good cause.

They headed away from the stalls further into the park before Jake took Echo's hearing helper dog coat off so he'd know that it was time for play. Then Jake took the squeaky ball Tony had given him out of his school bag and threw it as far as he could. 'Fetch, Echo, fetch!'

'Good throw!' said Tony.

Jake looked over at him to make sure Tony truly meant the words and wasn't just messing with him. But Tony's expression seemed to be genuine as he watched Echo race after the ball.

The little dog picked it up in his mouth and ran back with it; he dropped it at Jake's feet, skipped back a step, and then looked down at the ball and up at Jake with a wag of his tail. It was perfectly clear what he wanted.

Jake picked up the ball and gave it to Tony. 'Your turn.'

Tony threw the ball across the grass and Echo went tearing after it. But it wasn't Tony he brought it back to but Jake. Tony didn't seem to mind.

'You're really lucky to have a dog like Echo,' he said, as Jake threw the ball. 'Even if he wasn't a hearing dog, he'd be great on the cricket team!'

Jake laughed as Echo brought the ball back, dropped it and looked up at him, his head tilted to one side. Tony picked it up and threw it for him and Echo set off after it again, tail wagging like mad, and brought it back. Then he sat down in front of Jake, his eyes glued to the ball, willing it to be thrown.

Jake picked the ball up. 'Fetch, Echo!'

Echo didn't need to be asked twice. He was already racing after it as fast as he could before it even touched the ground, his tail wagging. He skidded to a halt just in front of it, grabbed the ball in his mouth and ran back with it to Jake and Tony and dropped it at Jake's feet.

'It's my turn again now,' Tony said.

But, when Tony threw the ball this time, it landed in one of the large rhododendron bushes close to the car park.

'Oops,' he said. The ball had gone further than he'd intended it to.

'Echo'll find it,' Jake reassured him. 'He's really good at sniffing out his ball when we play hide-and-seek at home. Wherever I hide it, he always manages to hunt it out.'

Echo raced into the rhododendron bush, determined to find the ball and take it back to Jake. But the ball had got caught on a branch and he whined and stretched up to try to reach it.

When he'd lived on the streets, Echo had needed to be aware of everything that was going on around him. Instantly alert to a movement in the corner of his eye, the sound of a step or a scent that only his super-sensitive nose could detect. But, since being trained as a hearing dog and living with Jake, he'd let his guard down. When people came up to him, he expected them to want to stroke him or give him a treat. When people spoke to him now, they did so with kind, gentle voices. It was what he'd become accustomed to.

So Echo wasn't thinking of anything other than retrieving the ball and taking it back to

Jake as he stood on his back legs and stretched up for it. But as he did so two large hands grabbed him and threw him into the boot of a car and slammed it shut.

'Echo!' Jake called, when he didn't come out of the bush. 'Echo, where are you?'

He never usually took this long to bring the ball back and now there was a car over by the bush. It must be part of the Fresh Start Festival, but Jake didn't want Echo to get run over.

'Echo!'

Echo barked and barked from inside the boot of the car.

'Stop that racket,' the man growled, and he turned the radio up as loud as it would go to try to drown out the sound of Echo's barking. He turned the key and pressed his foot down on the accelerator.

Jake didn't see or hear the car as he and Tony headed over to the bush where the ball had landed to help Echo find it.

'Look out!' Tony shouted. He pushed Jake to one side as the car that had been next to the rhododendron bush careered past them.

Jake stared at the car that had almost hit him as it drove on.

'My dad says drivers like that should be banned for life,' Tony said. 'Look – now he's going out of the entrance instead of the exit.'

'Pepsi,' Jake said.

'What?'

'The number plate – PEP 51,' Jake said over his shoulder, as he hurried over to the bush. 'Echo?' he said. 'Echo, where are you?'

He saw something in the grass and bent down to pick it up. Now Jake was frightened. 'Echo!' he shouted, as loudly as he could. 'ECHO!'

'What is it?' Tony said. 'What's happened?'

And Jake opened his hand to show him what he'd found inside the bush: Echo's squeaky ball.

'Where is he?'

'He was right here.'

'Where can he have gone?'

'Echo! ECHO!'

But, although both boys shouted as loudly as they could, Echo didn't come back.

'Do you think he went over there?' Tony said, pointing back to where the festival stalls were being erected.

'He might have gone to see if there was any food,' Jake said. He didn't think Echo would have done so, but he couldn't be absolutely sure. Helper dogs were trained not to take food unless it was given to them. But the smell of burgers and hot dogs had been very strong. Maybe too strong for a hungry little dog to resist.

Jake and Tony kept on looking all around for Echo as they headed back across the park.

'Excuse me, have you seen my dog?' Jake asked a man walking a poodle.

'It's a Border terrier cross about this big,' Tony said, putting a hand to his knee. But the man shook his head.

Tony ran over to some children playing football to ask them while Jake headed over to ask one of the gardeners. But no one had seen Echo.

'Let's try him,' Tony said, pointing to the man in the brown suit holding the clipboard, and Jake and Tony ran over to the festival site.

The man was directing the driver of a lorry pulling a carousel over to the left when Jake and Tony stopped in front of him.

'We're putting all the rides over there away from the stage,' the man was saying.

'Right you are, Mr Cooper,' said the driver.

'How can I help you?' the clipboard man asked Jake and Tony.

'It's my dog . . .'

'His hearing dog,' Tony interjected.

'He's gone missing.'

'What sort of dog is it?'

'A Border terrier cross.'

'He's tan-coloured.'

'I'll put an alert out for you, see if we can find him,' Mr Cooper said, looking concerned.

'I used to know one of those,' a woman said, handing Mr Cooper a mug of tea. 'Used to live with us under the old bridge.'

'This is a *hearing* dog, Jen,' Mr Cooper said. 'Not a stray.'

'He could hear fine, but he didn't like to be stroked until he got to know you. Bones we called him, didn't we, George?' she said to an elderly man wearing a red-and-white spotted bandana round his neck.

'Alerted me more than once when a skateboarder was heading in my direction,' George said.

But the last part of what Jen and George said was drowned out by Mr Cooper raising a megaphone and speaking into it and Jake wasn't looking at their faces to lip-read them.

'Everyone please be on the alert for a missing dog called . . .' He looked at Jake and raised an eyebrow.

'His name's Echo,' Tony said.

Mr Cooper raised the megaphone again. 'The dog's name is Echo. He's a tan Border terrier cross. Anyone seeing him should report to me immediately.'

'Thank you,' Jake said. It was getting late. His mum would be wondering where he was. But he didn't want to leave the park until he was absolutely sure Echo wasn't anywhere in it. Maybe he'd got himself caught on something or fallen down a hole. He might be injured.

Jake remembered the speeding car. Perhaps Echo had been run over! He started running back to the rhododendron bush and Tony ran after him. Maybe Echo was lying among the leaves, unconscious.

Jake felt sick as he ran. He should have checked inside the bush more thoroughly.

'Echo, Echo!' he cried, pushing his way through the thick foliage, dreading what he might find. Tony helped him look and they covered every bit of ground, but Echo wasn't there.

Jake was beside himself with worry as he phoned his mum. He dashed angrily at the tears that ran down his face. Crying wouldn't help. When she answered, he choked out the words: 'It's Echo – he's gone.'

'What do you mean, gone?' his mum said.

'One minute he was here and the next minute he wasn't. Mum, help – please. I don't know what to do.'

'Where are you?'

'At the park with Tony.'

'I'll be right there.'

'We'll keep on looking till you get here.'

Jake's mum brought Echo's box of gravy bones with her. 'I heard somewhere that they rattle treats to get dogs to come back,' she said, when she found the boys.

But, even though they looked all over the park again, and Jake called and called, while Tony shook the box of treats and asked everyone they passed, Echo didn't come back.

'Sometimes dogs get wanderlust,' Jake's mum said gently. 'He was a stray before Helper Dogs trained him after all.'

But Jake didn't believe that.

'He wouldn't run off. Not from me,' he said. 'He wouldn't, he couldn't . . . would he?' Doubt crept into Jake's voice. Maybe Echo didn't want to stay with him any more.

Jake's mum phoned Helper Dogs and the dog warden and the police.

'Sometimes dogs are stolen and driven far away so they can be tricky to find,' the dog warden told Jake's mum softly when she arrived at the park. She didn't mean for Jake to hear her, but he lip-read her.

Stolen! But who would want to steal Echo? And why?

Once the police arrived, they took down details about Echo and what had happened.

Suddenly Jake remembered the car that had been so eager to get out of the park that it drove through the entrance gate.

'He was in that car,' he said. 'The car that almost knocked me over. Why else was it stopped there?'

'Are you sure?' the policewoman asked him. 'Can you describe it?'

'Yes, I'm sure. It was a blue Ford Mondeo. The number plate was PEP 51.' He wasn't going to forget that in a hurry.

'He was driving like a maniac – almost knocked Jake over,' Tony said.

The policewoman nodded and then she turned back to Jake.

'But you don't have any proof? You didn't actually see your dog in the car?'

Jake shook his head and looked down at his feet. 'But where could Echo have gone if he wasn't stolen?' he said.

'It's time we were going home,' Jake's mum said, putting an arm round his shoulders.

But Jake shrugged her off. He refused to go until they'd done another sweep of the park and asked everyone they came across if they'd seen anything. But no one had. Eventually, they had to give up and go back to the car.

Jake stared out of the window as Mum started the engine. There were flags outside the new shelter for the homeless. People laughed as they ate cake off paper plates and drank juice from paper cups. There was a banner saying GRAND OPENING.

An old man wearing a tattered red-and-white spotted bandana round his neck caught

Jake looking and waved his paper cup at him. But Jake didn't wave back.

Vicky burst into tears when she heard the news. 'Poor Echo,' she cried.

Jake's mum phoned Dog Lost, the RSPCA and all the vets and dog rescue centres in the area. She watched as Jake put messages on Facebook and Twitter. They set up a page just for Echo and called it 'Echo, Come Home'.

Jake uploaded a photo of Echo holding the squeaky ball to it. 'Maybe someone's seen him. Maybe someone out there will be able to help.'

As the Ford Mondeo drove further and further away from the park, Echo stopped barking and began to whimper instead. But the man still had his radio on full blast and didn't hear him. Finally, Echo curled up in a small, frightened ball, his little body trembling.

Chapter 18

As soon as the car boot opened, Echo was ready and he leapt out.

'Hey – what – stop!' a voice yelled and a hand grabbed Echo's collar.

But Echo squirmed and twisted until the dognapper was holding a collar but no dog.

'Stop!' the man shouted, as he tried to grab him again.

But Echo wasn't stopping for anyone. He had to find Jake, but he wasn't in the park any more and he had no idea how to get home. Nowhere smelt even the least bit familiar. He ran on and on, desperate to get away from the man and find his way back to Jake. Down one street and up another, through an open gate and along an alleyway. Past a junkyard with a dog that barked at him. Over a footbridge and under an arch. On and on and on until finally he couldn't run any more and he slowed to a walk as the sky above grew grey and stormy.

It started to rain and Echo's head drooped. He wasn't frightened of thunder or lightning, like some dogs. But he hated the cold wetness of the rain. He crawled under some building rubble in a front garden to get away from it, but almost immediately he realized there was already something in there – a cat.

Only this cat wasn't like Jasper at Helper Dogs. It hissed and snarled as it swiped at him with its sharp claws. Echo crawled out from under the rubble and ran away.

Finally, exhausted and soaked through, he curled up by some industrial-sized dustbins at the back of a building, miserable and shivering with cold.

Jake's keen-eyed information about the car's make and number plate meant it wasn't long after Echo's escape that the police were knocking at the dognapper's door.

'What's this all about?' the man asked angrily. 'I haven't done anything wrong.'

'Were you at Addison Park earlier today, sir?' the policewoman asked him.

'No . . . Never been there . . .'

'We already know you were there, sir,' the policeman said mildly.

'So what if I was? It's a free country.'

'May we come in, please?'

Inside the house the two police officers found three miserable-looking dogs in a cage.

'They're my dogs,' the man insisted.

'Then you won't mind if we check their microchips,' the policeman said, as he dialled the number for the RSPCA.

'You've got no right,' the dognapper said.

'I think you'll find we do,' the policewoman told him.

She held up Echo's collar that she'd found thrown on the dresser. 'Would you mind explaining this, sir?'

The man saw what she had and gulped. 'Never seen it before in my life,' he said. 'You must have planted it on me!'

But they all knew he was lying.

'Where's Echo?' the policewoman demanded.

'Don't know what you're talking about,' the man said grumpily. 'This is police brutality, this is. I'll get my lawyer on to you . . .'

'The little dog that was wearing this collar,' the policewoman said, waving it in front of his nose.

'All right, all right, I did have him but he ran off. Slippery as an eel, that dog. He was running for the main road last I saw him. Been knocked down most likely and serve him right.'

The policeman and woman looked at each other and shook their heads.

A few minutes later, a man from the RSPCA arrived and checked the microchips of the dogs in the cage. All of them had been reported missing.

'I'll make sure they get safely home. Lucky for them they were all microchipped,' he said, as the dognapper looked daggers at him.

'I haven't done anything wrong. I *found* those dogs. I was looking after them!' the man said, and then he smirked because there was no one to say it wasn't true. The dogs couldn't talk.

The policewoman looked down at Echo's collar.

'What's the maximum penalty for theft from a public place?' she asked her partner.

'Seven years in prison.'

'You can't . . . I haven't . . .' the dogsnatcher said, looking from one to the other.

'And if there's blackmail or a ransom note involved?'

The dogsnatcher bit his lip as he looked over at the kitchen drawer. The policeman smiled. He pulled on a pair of latex gloves and opened it.

'What do we have here?' he said, pulling out three ransom notes.

'I've never seen them before in my life!' the dog thief shouted. But he looked really scared.

'Oh, I've just remembered,' the policewoman said. 'It's fourteen years when there's a ransom demand involved, isn't it?'

'If you wouldn't mind coming with us, sir,' the policeman said.

The dognapper's shoulders slumped as the handcuffs were put on him.

*

Lenny came round shortly after Jake had finished putting Echo's picture on the Dog Lost website.

'I heard what happened,' he said.

'I'm so sorry,' Jake said. 'One minute we were playing and the next . . .' His voice trailed off. Although he knew Lenny couldn't know the answer, he still had to ask: 'Do you think I'll get him back?'

Lenny frowned. 'That dog loves you,' he said. 'Plain as the nose on my face, and dogs like that . . .'

Jake swallowed hard. 'What about dogs like that?'

'They'll find a way to get back to the person they love or die trying,' said Lenny softly.

'I don't want Echo to die!' Jake said. 'I'd rather he lived with someone else than suffered trying to come home.'

Lenny nodded. 'I know you would. It's probably why he loves you so much.'

'I love him too,' Jake said.

'You're probably the first and only person who did. We loved him as well, of course. But you two had something special.'

A tear rolled down Jake's face as he choked out the words that were so hard to say.

'What if he wasn't stolen . . .? What if he ran away . . . because I did something wrong?'

Lenny shook his head firmly. 'No,' he said. 'That dog would never run away from you.'

'Jake, Jake!' Vicky shouted from the front door. 'The police are here!'

Jake and Lenny hurried to join her.

Jake's heart lifted and then sank when he saw that the police didn't have Echo with them.

'But we did find this,' the policewoman said, and she gave him Echo's collar.

Jake stared down at it. It looked so small and fragile. He swallowed hard and then looked back up at her as she explained that Echo had been dognapped, but had managed to escape.

'The patrol cars are keeping an eye out for him. Don't give up,' said the policeman and Jake nodded. He wouldn't give up. He'd never give up. At least now he knew Echo was out there somewhere. That he had definitely been taken. That he hadn't just run away.

'Where did you find the collar?' Lenny asked the police.

'Wellston.'

It was about thirty miles away, but Jake had never been there and neither, as far as he knew, had Echo. How was the little dog supposed to find his way home from there? It was impossible. Jake just hoped one of the patrol cars spotted him.

'We'll be in touch as soon as we hear anything,' the policewoman said, as she turned to leave.

Outside it was spitting with rain.

'Looks like we're in for a storm,' said Lenny.

When they'd all gone, Jake checked his hearing aids to make sure they were working. Everything was so hollow and empty without Echo there. It felt all wrong.

'You have to eat something,' Jake's mum said. 'A sandwich at least.'

But Jake just shook his head. He felt cold and numb as he went up to his room and lay on his bed.

'Echo, come home,' he whispered. 'Please come home.'

Now Echo was gone the tinnitus that used to fill his ears and his head came back with a vengeance and he couldn't fall asleep because it was so loud. It went on and on until finally he gave up trying and stared out of the window, wondering where Echo was and wishing that he'd come back.

Chapter 19

The residents of the old people's home weren't allowed to keep pets, although sometimes one of the staff brought their dog in to see them. Those were ninety-three-year-old Violet's favourite days.

She'd had dogs herself, all sorts of dogs – big and small, pedigrees and crosses, good dogs and little imps – for almost her whole life and she missed not having one more than she could say. Waggy tails and woofs had been her world until she couldn't manage to live on her own any more.

Now she had to make do with the plants on her windowsill. The geraniums and begonias were thriving, and she talked to them every day, but they just weren't the same as having a real-life pet.

The staff liked the old people to be in their rooms early each night – it made it easier for them to tidy up – and Violet didn't mind. She sat in her chair by the window and looked out across the grass. Then she remembered the bit of cake she'd saved from dinner for the birds.

The windows on the ground floor at the home didn't open as wide as normal windows for security reasons, but Violet's window opened just enough for her to put her hand through and crumble the cake on to the narrow ledge outside.

She knew the staff probably wouldn't approve if they knew what she was doing. Health and hygiene . . . rats . . . She could almost hear them telling her off.

Well, this time what the staff don't know won't harm them, Violet decided.

She must have dozed off in her chair because it was getting dark by the time she opened her eyes. She looked out of her window and did a double take. She couldn't believe it. There was a little dog standing there on its back legs and eating the cake she'd put out for the birds.

'Oh my,' she said. 'Oh my goodness,' and she pushed the window as far open as it would go. 'Come on in,' she said, and Echo hopped through.

'You all right, Violet?' one of the nurses said, tapping on her door.

Echo looked up at Violet and Violet put her finger to her lips. If the nurse knew the little dog were here, she'd take it away.

'Oh yes,' Violet said shakily. 'Quite all right, thank you. Just talking to myself. Night-night, dear.'

The nurse shook her head as she headed back the other way. Violet had always seemed very with it. She hoped the old lady wasn't starting to get confused.

'Hello there,' Violet whispered to Echo, as soon as the nurse had gone, and Echo wagged his tail. 'I expect you're thirsty. Let's have a nice cuppa.'

Violet made herself a cup of tea in the tiny kitchenette she had in her bedsit room, added two sugars to it and then poured some into a saucer for Echo.

Echo had never had tea before, but he lapped it up with his little pink tongue while Violet sipped her own tea and nodded.

'Nothing like a cup of tea to perk you up, is there?' she said.

Echo had finished his already. He sat down and held out a paw to Violet. His meaning was very clear to the old lady and Violet understood perfectly that Echo wanted more.

'And eggs,' Violet said. 'They're good too.'

She looked in her mini fridge and Echo came to investigate too. But she didn't have any eggs in there, just milk. Violet had most of her meals in the dining room with the other residents at the home, although she did have a small hotplate and saucepan for heating up soup and milky drinks. She'd hardly ever used it in the past year.

'Porridge,' Violet said. 'That'll fill you up, little dog.' She had oats and plenty of milk so she set about making Echo some sugary porridge in a saucepan on the hotplate while Echo watched her. Once it was done, she took the saucepan off the heat and spooned the gloopy mixture into a bowl. She put the saucepan back on the hotplate and waited for the porridge to cool. Echo whined.

'I know you're hungry,' Violet said. 'But you don't want to burn your mouth, do you?'

Echo sat down to wait, his eyes never leaving the bowl of porridge. At last, Violet decided it was cool enough for him to eat and set the bowl down in front of him.

He ate it all up and licked the bowl clean while Violet smiled at him.

'My little Tookie liked porridge too,' she told Echo. 'Especially if there was a bit of cream on top. Couldn't give him too much though because he wasn't a big dog. Only a little bit bigger than you. He was such a funny little thing. His curly poodle fur was almost the same colour as porridge.'

Echo's pink tongue came out to lick his lips.

'My Walter wouldn't touch oats, mind,' Violet continued. 'Acted as if porridge was poison if you put a bowl of it in front of him. But then Walter was a scavenging sort of dog and thought nothing of gulping down a raw rat.' Violet shuddered at the thought.

'So many dogs and cats and parrots and canaries over the years and all of them so different from each other with their own distinct personalities. I loved them all.'

Violet's eyes closed and she drifted off to sleep in her chair as she remembered the pets she'd loved. Echo lay on the rug beside her and went to sleep too.

It was a while later when the nurse made her rounds and saw the light still on under Violet's door.

'You OK in there, Violet?' she called, tapping at Violet's door but not opening it.

Violet blinked and looked down at Echo lying on the rug beside her. It hadn't been a dream. The little dog was really here.

The nurse knocked again. 'Violet?

'Yes, dear, just going to sleep. See you in the morning,' Violet called back.

'Sleep tight,' the nurse said.

'Don't let the bedbugs bite!' Violet replied cheerily. She used her walking frame to make her way to the bed and once she was in it she tapped the spot beside her and Echo jumped up on to it.

Violet sighed with happiness. She didn't quite know how she was going to keep the little dog a secret, but now it was here she very much wanted to keep it.

The old lady drifted off to sleep with a smile on her face and didn't give a thought to the saucepan she'd put back on the hotplate that was gradually getting hotter and hotter.

She was so tired that she didn't wake up as the smoke filled the room, but Echo did and he licked and whined and licked Violet's face some more until the old lady woke up too.

'It's not time for playing,' Violet said, but then she stopped talking and started to cough because of all the smoke.

She threw back the covers and reached for her walking frame next to the bed. But, just as she took hold of the handles, a second wave of coughing shook her and, as she tried to grasp the walker, she tumbled to her knees instead.

Echo barked and barked and ran to Violet, licking her face, wanting her to get up, but he wasn't strong enough to lift her.

'Do you hear a dog barking?' one of the nurses in the break room said.

'Sounds a lot like one to me,' said another nurse and they went to investigate just as the smoke alarm went off. They wouldn't have known the alarm had started in Violet's room if Echo hadn't kept on barking and led them to it.

'What's a dog doing in your . . .' the first nurse started to say, as Echo came running over to them, frantic with worry for Violet who was still lying on the floor.

'Oh, Violet!' the second nurse said, as they ran into the room. One of them scooped Violet up and carried her out while the other nurse grabbed a towel and pushed the saucepan off the hotplate and turned the switch off.

'We were only just in time,' they said to each other, once they were safely outside.

'If it hadn't been for that dog . . .'

The two nurses exchanged glances. Who knew what might have happened?

Violet looked very small, fragile and a bit dazed as she sat in an armchair while the nurse who had carried her out held her hand. Echo sat on the other side of her and Violet rested her hand on his little head.

'It's all right, Violet, you're safe now,' the nurse said.

The other nurse phoned the matron.

'I'll be there as soon as I've called the duty doctor,' she said.

'Thank you,' Violet said to Echo, as she stroked his soft, furry head. Her throat was sore from the smoke and her voice was hoarse.

Other residents came out of their rooms to see what was going on.

'Are we having a barbecue?'

'What's a dog doing here?'

'Hello, Champ.'

'He's like my old dog.'

'He saved me,' Violet told them, as the matron arrived.

The matron was not pleased to find a dog in the corridor. The home had a strict no-pets policy.

'What's it doing here?' she wanted to know.

But the nurses only shrugged and shook their heads. They didn't want Violet to be in trouble.

'He saved me,' Violet told the matron.

But the matron wasn't listening. She was staring at Echo. The little dog didn't have a collar and they couldn't have stray dogs wandering about the building. It might have fleas. Word would get round that the home was unhygienic.

'Go on now, shoo,' the matron said, waving her hands at the little dog.

Echo hesitantly stood up, not sure what was happening.

'Shoo!' the matron said again, and she picked up a magazine and shooed him all the way down the corridor and out of the back door.

She'd only just managed to shut him outside where they stored the dirty laundry in a lean-to when the duty doctor came in the front way.

'Hello, doctor!'

'Matron.'

The doctor listened to Violet's chest through his stethoscope.

'Try not to talk too much,' he said. 'Your throat may be sore for a few days because of the smoke.'

But Violet didn't listen to him. 'If it wasn't for that little dog, I wouldn't be here,' she croaked.

'What little dog?' the doctor asked.

'A stray,' the matron told him. 'Don't worry, I've sent it on its way.'

'He saved me,' Violet said, clasping the doctor's wrist.

'You should have called the RSPCA to check if it was microchipped,' the doctor told the matron, as he shone a light in Violet's eyes.

But she hadn't, thought Violet, and now Echo was gone.

The laundry lean-to that the home used to store dirty laundry, although covered from the rain, was open at the sides to the elements. Echo tried lying on the hard stone floor, but it wasn't as comfortable as Violet's bed. The porridge had made him thirsty and, as Echo was a very agile little dog, it was no problem at all to hop up on to the sink and lick at the dripping tap. Then he jumped down on top of the sheets and bedding and towels in the trolley that was waiting to be taken away by the laundry service the next day.

This new bed was much more comfortable than the floor and Echo buried himself deep down among the linen and was soon fast asleep.

Chapter 20

The first thing Jake noticed when he woke up was how empty his room felt without Echo in it. He'd got used to that furry face sharing his pillow. But not this morning.

He went downstairs and turned on the laptop on the table in the kitchen while his mum made him some toast.

First he clicked on the Dog Lost page to see if there'd been any sightings of Echo. Then he looked at the Facebook page he and his mum had created the evening before.

At 11 p.m. Tony's older sister, Tara, had shared Jake's post about Echo having been stolen on her own Facebook page.

One of Tara's Facebook friends was Li, whom she went to college with, when he wasn't working at his dad's Chinese restaurant.

Li was horrified to learn that Echo had been stolen and could now be wandering around lost thirty miles away in Wellston. It was so unfair. After everything he'd been through, he'd finally found a home, but now he was back out on the streets. Li shared Jake's post with his 1,003 friends and added the photo that he'd taken of Echo eating noodles.

It was such a cute, funny photograph that it and Jake's original post were passed on from friend to friend until Echo's picture had been seen all across the world and back again.

'Mum,' Jake said, looking up from the computer, confused. 'Mum . . . I don't understand . . .'

Under the original post that Jake had put up about Echo being missing, and then the second one where he'd added that they now knew the little dog had been stolen and had escaped, hundreds of people had posted comments. Everyone wanted to offer advice or sympathy or to try to help him find Echo.

'*We know how it feels. We lost our dog . . .*'

'*Have you tried shaking Echo's biscuits around the neighbourhood . . .*'

'*Might not have gone far . . .*'

'*We're thinking of you . . .*'

'*Hope you hear something soon . . .*'

'*Dognappers should be sent to jail . . .*'

The comments went on and on.

'I didn't know so many people would care about him,' Jake said, his voice catching in his throat.

Jake's mum squeezed his shoulder, as she brushed away the tears that rolled down her face. The response was overwhelming.

The local breakfast news was on the TV and Jake's mum turned round quickly when one of the two newscasters said the word 'Echo'.

On the screen was Li's picture of the little dog eating noodles.

'Finally, we'd like everyone to be on the lookout for this little chap,' the newscaster said. 'His name's Echo and he's a hearing helper dog . . .' Up popped a picture of Echo in his hearing helper dog coat.

'He was stolen from Addison Park yesterday afternoon at around four p.m. The thief took him to a house in Wellston where the brave little chap managed to escape, leaving his collar behind. Anyone who has any information that could be helpful should inform the police or the dog warden or Helper Dogs. Echo belongs to a young man called Jake Logan.'

'I bet Jake's really missing him,' the other newscaster said. 'Come home soon, Echo.'

Jake and his mum both jumped when the kitchen door swung open.

'Dad!' Jake cried.

'Heard what happened so I came back,' his dad said, pulling Jake into a hug. He held him tight as Jake let the tears that had been stinging his eyes fall.

'I can't bear it,' he sobbed.

'We'll find him, son,' his dad said. 'Someone must know something. What have you done so far?'

Jake and his mum told him.

'Posters?' his dad asked.

'Yes. For Dog Lost. The posters are great and they've been really helpful.'

'We should make posters to put up all over town and then all the way up to Wellston,' his dad said. 'Is it a clear photo of Echo on the Dog Lost posters, Jake?'

'Yes.'

'Good. Let's get printing.'

'How many shall I do?'

'A hundred to start off with. No, better make it two hundred.'

Jake's mum put the kettle on while they did the printing. Once his dad had drunk a quick cup of tea, he and Jake set off.

They were putting a poster up on a lamp post in the centre of town when a voice said: ''Scuse me.'

Jake looked round to see a dishevelled man with a beard heading towards him. He looked up at his dad.

'Can I help you?' Jake's dad said.

The man reached into his coat and pulled out a crumpled bit of paper. He held it out to Jake. 'For you.'

Jake took the paper and looked down at the drawing on it.

'Echo,' he gasped, as he stared at the pencil sketch. It was definitely Echo's little furry face, although his coat was longer. Jake would know that funny, quizzical look anywhere. 'Have you seen him? Do you know where he is?'

The man shook his head. 'Haven't seen him in months. Just went off one morning and never came back. We used to call him Bones because that's what he liked to eat whenever one of us could afford one.'

'Did you used to collect money outside the supermarket?' Jake asked slowly. He remembered a homeless man being there one day. He had had a dog with him. A dog that had looked a bit like Echo now he thought about it, but with a longer, straggly coat.

'There and a few other places. George mostly did the collecting with him outside the supermarket. That was his spot. I'm Harvey, by the way. Sometimes − not always − Bones came to sleep under the old bridge with us and I welcomed his company. So did the others that used to sleep there before it was demolished.'

'Where are you sleeping now?' Jake's dad asked, reaching into his pocket for some money. But Harvey wouldn't take it.

'Keep it,' he said. 'We've got a new home now. The Fresh Start Hostel over by the park. Never thought I'd have a proper roof over my head again, but it's OK and they give us lockers and a padlock so our things are safe.' He breathed in noisily and then smiled. 'Good food too. They're trying to organize a fishing trip to the river and all sorts of other activities. Don't think I'll join in though. Not much of a joiner-in . . . But George will. George likes fishing.'

'Will you keep a lookout for Echo?' Jake said. 'He's my hearing dog and now he's missing. He could be anywhere from here to Wellston.'

Harvey nodded. 'Will do and I'll ask the others at the hostel too.'

'Thank you,' said Jake's dad and Jake nodded.

Soon all the takeaway restaurants on Echo's old feeding road had put posters in their windows.

'When he comes back, I'm giving him one super-deluxe, extra-large noodle meal on the house,' Li said.

He looked at Jake's sad face. 'Hang on in there,' he said.

'I will.'

'Now all we need to do is put more posters up from here to Wellston,' Jake's dad said.

Vicky and her friends, plus Mum and the volunteers from Dog Lost, helped to put up the posters everywhere they could. Tony and Tara lent a hand too while Lenny shared the information about Echo being stolen on different assistance dog charity websites.

Jake couldn't believe that so many people would want to help or care so much. It gave him a strange feeling inside. Not a bad feeling, just an unfamiliar one. He, and Echo, had lots more friends than he'd ever imagined and every one of them wanted to help.

'We'll bring some more paper with us tomorrow,' Tony said.

'And ink. We're running low on that too,' said Tara, as they headed off with another stack of posters.

'Thanks,' Jake said.

He'd spoken to far more people since Echo had gone missing than he usually did in months, but there were still no definite sightings of the little dog by the end of the day.

Jake was determined to do everything he could to find Echo.

'What are you doing?' Vicky asked him, when they were finally all at home and waiting for the takeaway Dad had ordered.

'Printing out a map so we can mark any sightings of Echo,' Jake told her.

The dog warden had told Jake that when dogs were lost they tended to travel in a triangle trying to find their way home. She'd explained to him that the triangle could sometimes be miles long.

'Good idea,' said Jake's dad.

'I'm going to use red pins for definite, or almost definite and most likely, sightings. All other colours for possibles but not so definite.'

Jake put the first red pin in Addison Park because it was the last place Echo had been seen. And the second one in the centre of Wellston. He sighed. Echo was so very far from home.

Chapter 21

It was six o'clock in the morning when the laundry-service truck arrived. Echo was fast asleep, deep down among the sheets, pillowcases and towels, but he woke up as soon as the trolley wheels started moving.

The next moment there was an electrical whirring sound as Echo peeped out from the top of the sheets. His stomach flipped as he felt the trolley going upward.

His paws scrabbled to get a footing among the pillowcases. He was just about to jump out of the trolley when the whirring sound stopped and the laundry truck door slammed shut. He was trapped inside!

Echo whimpered in the darkness as the truck drove off, but had to stay where he was. When the truck stopped ten minutes later, he was still hidden among the dirty washing.

He didn't move as the trolley was taken off the truck and into the industrial laundry. Finally, when the trolley had stopped and he'd listened for a long while to make sure there was no one about, he started scrambling among the sheets, pushing them this way and that as he made his way to the top.

Only Echo was wrong about there being no one about.

The woman loading the washing into the machines saw the linen in the trolley from the old people's home moving about. She screamed and grabbed a long-handled mop and started hitting the trolley with it.

'A rat! A rat!' she cried.

Echo's front paws reached past the top sheet and the next second he nimbly jumped out of the trolley, avoiding the mop. The woman stared at him in amazement and breathed a sigh of relief. Not a rat after all, but a lovely little dog.

'*He-llo*,' she started to say, but Echo was already racing out of the laundry room, up the driveway, through the gates and away down the street.

He ran past the tree with a cat sitting among the branches, looking down at him, over the road with a drain smelling of sour milk, through the bushes where a hedgehog lived, down an alley where a dog barked from behind a fence and out on to the street on the other side.

A police patrol car spotted him a few minutes later.

'Tom, stop!' the policeman said to the driver. 'That looks like the lost dog my daughter showed me on Facebook. Let's get a closer look.'

Tom swerved to the side and pulled up. Echo looked warily over as the car door opened.

'Here, dog, here,' Tom said.

'His name's on the tip of my tongue,' the other policeman said. 'It's . . .'

But Echo didn't wait to hear the policeman say his name. As the other one edged towards him, the little dog stepped back and then turned and ran into the park as the two policemen chased after him.

'Stop!'

'Wait!'

They did their best, but they were no match for a streetwise little dog.

Echo had remembered everything he'd learnt as a stray dog living on his wits and instinct and now he used it all to avoid being caught.

Voices calling to him were ignored. Hands stretching out to him were shunned. When he stopped to drink from a puddle, he was on the alert for the slightest movement. If anyone came close, he was ready to run.

More and more sightings of Echo were reported back to Jake and there were soon lots of red pins on his map. But no one had found Echo by Sunday night.

Jake didn't want to go to school on Monday and his mum let him stay home.

'Just for today.'

At lunchtime, the postman rang the front doorbell.

'It's addressed to Echo,' Mum said, bringing in a parcel.

Inside was a ball and a note from a complete stranger saying, 'This is for Echo when he comes home.'

'Oh, that's really kind,' Mum said, as Jake read the note to her. 'They must have seen the photo of Echo with his ball that you put on Facebook.'

'He'll love playing with this when he comes back,' Jake said. He didn't look up at his mum because his eyes were blurry with tears.

But apart from the parcel there was no other news about Echo. Jake squeezed Echo's ball over and over, liking the way it sprang back to life when he pressed it.

Downstairs Vicky put her fingers in her ears. 'That sound is driving me crazy! I'm going to tell him to stop,' she said.

But Vicky's mum shook her head. 'He's not annoying you on purpose. He can't hear it.'

Finally, Jake stopped when he came down to check if there were any more sightings of Echo. There were but none of them seemed very likely. Some were even in different countries.

He looked at the Dog Lost website and then posted on Echo's Facebook page:

'*Still looking* ☹'

Comments came back almost immediately.

'*Don't give up!*'

'*You'll find him.*'

'*Our dog came back to us after being missing for five years . . .*'

Jake yawned and rubbed at his tired eyes. He didn't want to go to bed without Echo being there. But Jake's mum reminded him he had to go back to school the next day.

'Don't worry, I'll let you know if I hear anything,' she said. 'Anything at all.'

Chapter 22

Echo followed the river all through the starry, moonlit night. It took him past moored barges and rowing boats as it led him away from Wellston town centre. Gradually, the houses and back gardens he passed gave way to factories and warehouses as he reached the outskirts of the town and finally the countryside beyond. At first, his paws trod on paved river pathways, then rough stony ground, until finally there was no path.

The early-morning dew soaked Echo's paws and the fur on his short legs as he made his way through the overgrown grass along the riverbank. His paws were sore and his legs ached.

The sun was high in the sky when a dog barked and Echo stopped. He looked over at the wooded copse where the sound had come from. The bark wasn't that of a happy dog playing, or an angry dog, or even a warning. This bark was something quite different: it was a desperate cry for help.

Echo ran into the copse to find the dog that had made it. He didn't have to go far into the trees before he found an elderly German shepherd dog. He had been tied to a post and the string had become wound tightly round him as he'd desperately tried to break free.

The dog had stopped barking and was now howling in hopeless despair instead. He was so tangled up in the string that he could barely move and his grey-whiskered muzzle couldn't bite through it. His old eyes saw Echo coming towards him. He tried to wag his tail in greeting, but even that was caught up in the string. Echo looked up into the sad, desperate dog's eyes and wagged his own tail in greeting. He put his nose to the other dog's and then licked his furry face to tell him not to worry.

Echo walked round the dog, looking at the string, as the old dog whined. The string was thick and strong, but that didn't stop Echo. He tugged one end of it with his teeth, and kept on tugging, until the knot came unravelled, toppling Echo over as it suddenly came loose.

The old dog tried to reach out to him, but could only just touch him with his right front paw.

Echo jumped up and grasped the string in his teeth again. It didn't take long for him to lead the exhausted older dog round the tree a few times so he was free of the post, but not of the string round his neck, which trailed along behind him as he walked.

The two dogs sniffed at each other as the old dog's tail wagged and wagged and he licked Echo's face, happy to be free at last. A moment later, the two dogs heard someone crashing through the bushes towards them.

The old dog looked at Echo and whimpered. He was shaking with fear as the man headed towards them. The old dog lay down submissively as he towered over him, holding a stick. But Echo didn't cower, despite being less than half the size of the other dog.

He ran at the man, barking and growling, and as the man swung the stick towards Echo he raced out of the way. Then Echo started barking again and running back and forth, taunting the man as he ran from side to side while the man tried unsuccessfully to hit him with the stick.

Meanwhile the old dog, still on his belly, crept further away, back towards the river.

Finally, the man gave up trying to catch Echo – the little dog was too quick for him – and turned his attention back to the old dog instead. The poor dog looked behind him, saw the man coming and ran off with his tail between his legs. Echo barked at the man as if to say, '*I'm over here!*'

The little dog raced towards the man and then swerved away as the man swung the stick at him, growing angrier and angrier.

The old dog was now almost at the riverbank and ahead of him lay the water. He looked back at the man, terror in his eyes, as the man headed after him and raised the stick. Echo raced in between the man's legs once again and, as he swung the stick downwards at the little dog's head, the man toppled over and fell down the riverbank into the water below.

The old dog looked down at the man now splashing furiously in the river and gave one almost laugh-like bark. But, before the man could reach the bank and clamber out, the dogs had already raced off into the distance.

Chapter 23

As they left the man far behind, the old dog's steps became jauntier and his tail began to wag. At a spot where the riverbank was less steep the old dog took a long, cool drink of water before he lay down, panted for a little while and fell fast asleep.

Echo looked over at him and whined. The river's winding path lay ahead. He wanted to move on, but the old dog didn't wake up. So Echo lay down and slept too, a long, fitful, twitching sleep.

When Echo finally opened his eyes in the late afternoon, he could see the old dog was already awake. The little dog jumped up and gave himself a shake as the old dog staggered to his feet too, his tail gently wagging.

Together they made their way further into the countryside along the riverbank. Echo backed away when curious sheep and lambs came running over to him. But the old dog made reassuring noises deep in his throat as the sheep surrounded them. Echo's instinct was to run away from the white woolly creatures making strange noises, but the old dog's wagging tail showed him there was nothing to be afraid of.

Over the other side of the field there were two horses and a donkey eating grass, but when they saw Echo and the old dog they came over to say hello too. The horses put their great heads over the fence and Echo shied away in fear, but the old dog didn't. So Echo came back and sniffed at the animals too.

Next to the field was a small farmyard and Echo and the old dog went into it. Somewhere, not far away, Echo heard someone singing and his tail wagged. But before he could meet the singer he heard a squeak and stopped. It was the squeak of the ball that he and Jake used to play with. The squeak of happy times and fun. Echo gave a whimper and the next second he was running in the direction that the sound had come from with the old dog following along behind him, not sure what was going on.

Echo was almost bursting with excitement. Jake was here! He must be because that was the sound of the ball and Jake always, always had the squeaky ball.

The old dog nearly bumped into him as Echo came to a sudden stop.

Jake wasn't there. The squeak hadn't come from the ball. It had come from the goats playing in the corner of the yard and the noise was the creak of an old rocking chair that they were jumping on. There were three of them and Echo soon found out that the other farm animals they'd just met were much calmer than goats. Especially baby pygmy goats.

The mother goat was lying down on some hay in a stall, but the two baby goats were in constant motion, chasing each other, jumping on things, climbing up and down bits of wood. They never stopped moving and their tails wagged constantly. They danced round the old dog as, tired out from their journey, he went to lie down next to the mother goat. But they wouldn't let Echo get away so easily. He was just the right size to be their new playmate and they desperately wanted to have fun with him.

One of them ran at him, pretending to headbutt him, but when Echo scuttled away it only made them want to chase after him. Then it was his turn to chase them. They were very springy. Sometimes they stood up on their back legs and nearly did somersaults as they sprang about.

Echo was exhausted as the afternoon turned into evening, but when he tried to lie down the goats pushed at him with their heads and tapped him with their hooves. Echo moved but wherever he went they wanted to follow him. At last, he headed into the donkey stable. The baby goats didn't follow him in there, but the old dog did.

The hay bedding was sweet-smelling and fresh and the two dogs lay down at the far end and were soon fast asleep. They didn't stir when the donkey-stable door was closed for the night.

The next morning the chickens hurried out into the sunshine and Echo and the old dog followed them. The chickens were pecking at bits of corn and grains in the grass. One of them pecked up a worm and another chicken tried to take it as the first chicken ran across the grass, holding the worm in its beak.

Echo looked up into the sky as a plane flew through the clouds far up above. When the chickens saw it, they raced back into the chicken house and didn't come out again until it had gone far away. Then, one by one, they popped their heads out of the door and checked it was safe to come out before carefully placing one clawed foot after another on the wooden ramp of the chicken house. Soon all the chickens were back pecking at the grass.

Suddenly Echo heard a splash followed by a cry and then more splashing and a desperate bleating. One of the baby goats had somehow ended up in a large plastic barrel that was used to collect rainwater, and it was struggling to stay afloat. The other baby goat was bleating too as the mother goat tried to knock the water barrel over. Even though she was butting it with her head again and again, it was too heavy for her to topple.

Echo barked and barked and when no one came he went running to find help.

'Well, Gloria, I must say you're looking exceptionally beautiful this morning,' Louise told the large black-and-pink pig, as she showered her with warm water from the hosepipe.

Gloria grunted, as if she were agreeing with her. Louise picked up the brush and scrubbed softly at Gloria's bristled skin.

Echo came running up to them, barking.

'Well, hello there,' Louise said brightly, when she saw Echo with the old dog behind him. 'Word's got around I see.'

She'd been running this sanctuary for a few years now and these weren't the first animals that had turned up by themselves, although more often they were brought in by people who'd either rescued them or couldn't look after them any more for one reason or another. The sanctuary was really for rescued farm animals, but they did get the occasional cat or dog as well.

The young dog seemed full of energy. But the old dog definitely looked like he could use some TLC and they'd come to just the right place for that.

The old dog pushed his head under Louise's hand for a stroke and she happily obliged.

Echo put his paw on Louise's leg, as he'd been taught, but Louise didn't understand what he meant and stroked him instead. Echo whined and then moved away and barked, and at last she stood up and followed him. As they neared the rainwater barrel, Louise could see something was very wrong. She ran over to it and reached in, pulling the sodden, exhausted baby goat out.

'It's OK, it's OK. You're all right,' she said, holding it close to her as its little body trembled.

'What a good dog you are,' she said to Echo, and Echo wagged his tail as the old dog came forward and pushed his head under Louise's hand for another stroke.

Louise sat down on a haystack with the little goat and rubbed him with handfuls of hay to warm him up.

Half an hour later, the little goat was back playing with his brother, but the water barrel now had its lid securely on and Louise had put a box on top of it to make doubly sure it was safe. If the little dog hadn't come to fetch her, she dreaded to think what might have happened to Billy.

Chapter 24

'Hungry?' Louise asked the two dogs. She was sure that the older one must be. He was far too thin and had bald patches where he'd lost fur.

They'd just had two sacks of dog biscuits donated to them that morning, but the old dog's teeth wouldn't be able to crunch them up. She'd need to soak them in some gravy first so they got nice and soft.

Louise also looked after chickens that had come from the battery farm. They wore little jumpers that volunteers had knitted to keep them warm until their feathers grew back.

They had laid three eggs in the barn, which was a good sign. Louise didn't eat eggs herself, but she thought the dogs might like some for breakfast.

Echo watched as the pig waded into a muddy pond and rolled over in it, getting covered in muck. He gave a small, involuntary whine as if he couldn't understand why any creature would want to do that.

'Come on then,' Louise said, getting up from the hay bale she'd been sitting on. Echo stopped watching the pig and ran after the old dog and the friendly lady.

Once the old dog had finished his softened food and had a long drink of water, he lay down in a sunny spot and drifted off to sleep. Louise smiled as she watched his chest rise and fall. He looked quite at home already.

'Hercules,' she said to herself. It seemed like a good name for him. If he didn't have a name already, of course. She'd get one of the volunteers from Dog Lost to check if either of the dogs were microchipped, but if the old one didn't have a chip and didn't belong to anyone then she was going to name him Hercules. He had to be about thirteen years old and he looked like he was part of the sanctuary already.

By the time she'd seen to the geese, she'd decided for sure. She wasn't going to put Hercules up for adoption if no one came forward to claim him: this would be his home for the rest of his life.

'But this can't be your home, little Sprite,' Louise told Echo, who was following her around as she did her chores. 'Someone's bound to want a lovely little dog like you.'

Hercules looked a lot better after some good food and lots of sleep and his fur shone after his bath. He'd loved being dried! But when she tried to give Echo a bath he ran off towards the cow field.

'It's all right. You don't have to have a bath if you don't want to,' Louise called after him. And Echo stopped running and came back.

'Now let's take your pictures,' Louise said, pulling out her phone. There was a chance someone might be missing both dogs and she had to give them every opportunity to claim them.

Hercules' picture was easy to take, but little Sprite kept moving about so Louise wasn't able to get a good one and even her best effort was still blurry.

'Oh well, it'll have to do for now,' she said, as she used her phone to email the photo to the Dog Lost website. 'I'll try and get a better one when you're asleep and keeping still for once.'

Echo wagged his tail.

Every afternoon when he got home from school Jake found that the postman had brought more and more squeaky balls as well as other toys for Echo. But, before he opened the presents, Jake always checked the internet to see if there'd been any new possible sightings.

Today there was a blurred photo of a dog that looked a little bit like Echo, only it was hard to tell because the dog must have moved while it was being photographed. It had been taken by someone from the Home to Roost farm animal sanctuary only ten miles away.

'It could be him, Mum. It really could,' Jake said, as his mum squinted at the picture.

'Maybe,' she said doubtfully.

She tried ringing the sanctuary, but no one answered the phone. So she left a message, but that wasn't enough for Jake.

'We could be too late, Mum . . .'

Jake's mum sighed. She'd had a long day at work and the photo was such poor quality. It was impossible to tell if it were Echo or not. She opened her mouth to say no when she saw the desperate look on Jake's face.

'OK,' she said, as she picked up the car keys. 'Come on then.'

Dawn, the nearest Dog Lost volunteer, arrived at the sanctuary to see if the dogs were microchipped.

'No microchip on this one,' Dawn said, once she'd carefully checked the old dog's fur. 'His teeth are a bit of a mess and his breath isn't pretty,' she added, as the old dog panted. 'He's much too thin and his coat's terrible.'

Louise didn't mind about any of that. Hercules was home. And it was time for his friend to be home too.

'Sprite!' she called. 'Sprite – where are you? He was here just a minute ago.'

They looked everywhere but Echo had gone.

Jake had never been to a farm animal sanctuary before and he didn't quite know what

260

to expect as they drove through the gates of Home to Roost a short while later.

His stomach felt all swirly as he thought about finding Echo. He hoped so very much that the dog in the picture was him.

'Hello there,' Louise said, as they got out of the car.

She had Gloria the giant pig right behind her as she made her evening rounds. Jake was a bit worried about Gloria, but Louise told him that Gloria was very gentle and wouldn't hurt a fly.

Jake's mum told Louise they were there about the dog she'd taken a photo of.

'The big one or the little one?' Louise asked.

'The little one,' Jake said. He hadn't known there were two.

Louise's face fell. 'I'm so sorry,' she said. 'When Dawn came to check the dogs' microchips, we couldn't find little Sprite anywhere. I think he must have run off.'

She told them how Sprite had saved one of the baby pygmy goats from drowning. How the little dog had raced to fetch her, put a paw on her leg and led her over to where the baby goat had got himself trapped in the rainwater barrel.

'Those little goats are into everything,' Louise said, rolling her eyes. 'They just have no fear.'

'It had to have been Echo,' Jake said. 'He's a trained hearing dog and that's what they do. They put their paws out to alert someone in case they can't hear. It must have been him.'

But Jake's mum wasn't quite so sure. 'Other dogs could do that too,' she said.

'It was him,' Jake insisted, his voice catching in his throat. He had to believe it was because that might mean that one day, somehow, Echo would come back to him. 'Maybe he's still here somewhere. Maybe he hasn't gone.'

He turned away so they couldn't see his face and how upset he was. But it was devastating to know that he had only just missed him.

'We can look again,' Louise said, and Jake and his mum followed her as she made her way round the sanctuary, looking in all the barns and hiding places she could think of. 'Fewer than a quarter of the people who come to look at the animals ever take one home with them,' Louise said sadly.

'I know what it's like not to be picked,' Jake said.

Louise nodded. 'Sometimes it's not fair, is it?'

An old horse put its head over the fence and Jake ran his hand along its face.

'He's lovely,' he said.

'They all are,' Louise smiled. 'Most of them were going to be put down, or eaten, when they ended up here. I'm not even sure where some of them came from – they just turned up. One of the sheep was tied to my gate and I still don't know who put her there, but I'm very glad they did. Aren't I, Woolly?'

Woolly nuzzled Louise's hand to see if she had any treats.

'The only problem is the more animals I get, the harder it is to look after them all,' Louise added.

'I could help,' Jake said. 'And I bet my friend Tony would too.' Maybe Miss Dawson would even be able to make helping at the farm sanctuary a class project once the dog one was finished.

Jake paused by the chicken coop as something unexpected caught his eye.

'Erm . . . why are those chickens wearing jumpers?' he asked.

Chapter 25

It was twilight as Echo ran across the wasteland. Ahead of him, beyond the wide road, lay a river, and rivers led to home. He ran down the grassy bank and was halfway across the road when a huge lorry came bearing down on him and there was no time to run. He lay down flat on the tarmac as the lorry drove right over him and then swerved to the side with a squeal of brakes.

'Oh no. No!' the driver cried, as he stopped the lorry and jumped out. The little dog was lying very still. If it stayed where it was in the road, it was in danger of being run over again. The motorway was no place for a dog. No place for someone on foot either. Especially at twilight when drivers were only just starting to put on their headlights and oncoming vehicles weren't always so easy to spot.

The lorry driver checked and double-checked for traffic before running into the road and scooping up the little dog and hurrying back to the lorry with him. At least he couldn't see any blood.

If the dog were really lucky, the lorry had gone right over him without touching him. The wheels were so big and the bottom of the lorry was so high off the ground that there was a chance it could have done. The dog would have surely been killed instantly if any of the wheels had struck him.

He could feel the dog's heart beating fast and his little body was trembling. The driver sighed with relief: he definitely wasn't dead.

The lorry driver laid the little dog carefully on the seat next to him and drove home. It wasn't far, although it was dark by the time he parked up.

'What have you got, Dad?' his children, a boy and girl of six and seven, called Ben and Abby, wanted to know as the lorry driver carried the little dog into the house.

'Not another stray, Frank,' his wife said wearily, as she patted the back of the crying baby she held in her arms. He'd brought a cat home a few weeks ago and the children were so sad when Whiskers had left of his own accord through the cat flap a few days later.

'I found him on the motorway,' their dad told the children, as he put Echo down on the sofa.

'Is he OK?' asked Abby.

'I think so. He's probably just in shock,' her dad said.

Echo's tail flapped up and down once as Abby gently stroked his furry head.

'Get him some water and maybe a bit of cheese, Ben.'

Echo didn't want any water, although he did manage a nibble of cheese before falling fast asleep.

'I think he's OK,' Frank said, biting at his thumbnail.

'Doesn't seem to be in any pain,' said his wife, Mary.

'I'll take him to the vet's and try to find out who he belongs to tomorrow.'

'He's snoring,' Ben said, and Abby grinned. The snores were pretty loud for such a little dog.

Frank came down twice in the night to check on Echo. The first time the little dog was still asleep. But the second time he was awake so Frank took him outside. As he watched the dog sniffing the bushes before doing his business,

Frank was relieved to see that he didn't seem to be seriously injured in any way.

The next morning the children woke up to find the little dog was much livelier.

'Let's call him Ruffles,' said Abby.

'No, Waggy,' said Ben. 'He's always wagging his tail.'

'Heads it's Ruffles and tails it's Waggy,' their dad said, as he threw a coin up into the air and caught it. 'Waggy it is!'

They didn't have any dog food so they gave him the cat food they'd bought for Whiskers instead. Echo thought it was delicious.

Frank took a photo of him licking his lips when it was all gone and posted it on Facebook.

The baby started to cry and Echo looked over at it in its carrycot and then ran over to Mary, put out his paw to her and whined.

'What's going on?' she said.

'I think he's letting you know the baby's crying, Mary,' Frank said.

'How does he know to do that?' asked Abby.

'He's the cleverest dog in the world,' said Ben. 'And now he's our dog.'

'He'll only be our dog once we've taken him to the vet's so he can be checked for a microchip,' their dad reminded them. 'Someone could be out there right now desperately searching high and low for him.'

The children nodded, as they gave each other a look. They knew the dog might belong to someone else, but they couldn't help hoping that he didn't and could stay with them.

'Can we come?' Abby asked.

'OK.'

Mary looked at baby Charlie, fast asleep in his carrycot. If she got a move on, she might just have time for a quick shower before he woke up again. Then she and the baby could go on the outing too. She ran up the stairs and turned on the water.

'Dad, Whiskers is in the garden!' Ben said, pointing out of the window.

Dad, Ben and Abby went out to try to coax the cat back inside.

Echo lay next to the baby and when Charlie started crying again he knew just what he had to do. He ran up the stairs and put his paw on the bathroom door, but it was shut. He whined, but Mary didn't open it.

She was just lathering the shampoo in her hair when the little dog started barking outside the bathroom door. She tried to ignore it, but he just wouldn't stop.

'Shh, you bad dog!' she said, opening the door.

Echo stopped barking and now she could hear Charlie crying downstairs. She grabbed a towel and ran to him.

'It's OK, Charlie, Mummy's here.'

Abby, Ben and their dad came back inside, having been unable to catch Whiskers.

'I thought you were watching Charlie,' Mary said crossly.

'Sorry, love. We spotted Whiskers in the garden. He's come home!'

She looked down at Waggy. He gazed back up at her with his beautiful brown eyes.

'Good dog,' she smiled. 'Good dog!'

Frank took Charlie from her and she went to finish her shower and get ready. But, when it was time to leave for the vet's, Waggy wasn't there any more.

Echo had slipped through the cat flap and disappeared.

In the holidays, when Jake went with his dad on the long-haul trips, he liked sitting high up in the cab, looking out at the world rushing by, and they would play I Spy. But the only thing Jake wanted to spy now was Echo.

His dad was hoping to distract him from thinking about that so he took him along to get the lorry serviced. He'd told everyone he knew about Echo being missing. All of the other lorry drivers had promised to keep an eye out for him.

They were almost at the garage when Dad's phone rang.

'You still looking for that missing dog?' Dad's friend Bill said over the hands-free lorry-cab phone. 'I think we might have found him.'

Dad looked at Jake. 'You have. Where is he?'

Jake could hardly breathe. He so wanted someone to have found Echo.

'Frank Perkins picked up a dog on the motorway matching the description yesterday. And there's another thing . . .'

'Yes?'

'He alerted them to the sound of their baby crying.'

'That's what hearing dogs are trained to do!'
Jake cried.

They got Frank's address and it turned out to
be only a few miles away. Dad turned the lorry
round and headed to Frank's house. As soon as
they got there, Jake jumped down from the
cab, ran up the path and rang the doorbell. Echo
had to be here. He had to have finally found him.

Frank Perkins opened the door with Abby
and Ben right behind him.

'Where is he?' Jake asked them. 'Where's
Echo?'

Frank looked at Jake's dad as he came up
the path and shook his head. Jake's dad
squeezed Jake's shoulder.

'Who's Echo?' asked Abby.

'My dog,' said Jake.

'He means Waggy,' said Ben.

'He's gone,' Frank said.

'Went out through the cat flap,' said Mary.

'No, he can't be gone, he can't!' Jake cried.

'When did he go?' Jake's dad asked.

'Only a few hours ago.'

'He could still be around.'

Frank shook his head. 'We looked everywhere but we couldn't see him.'

Jake was devastated. 'But where can he have gone?' he said.

'Maybe it wasn't Echo,' his dad said. 'Maybe it was another dog.'

Frank pulled his phone from his pocket and showed them the photo he'd taken after Waggy had eaten the cat food.

'That's Echo,' Jake said miserably. He couldn't believe how close he'd been again to finding the little dog. They'd only missed him by a few hours.

'I couldn't just leave him on the motorway,' said Frank.

'The motorway!' Jake said, and now he was really worried. 'What was Echo doing on the motorway?'

'I don't know how he got there, but I ran right over him with my lorry. Luckily, the wheels are so big that its undercarriage is way off the ground and passed over him without hurting him.'

But it could have done, Jake thought to himself.

'I wish he'd stayed,' said Abby.

'You wouldn't have thought he'd be able to squeeze through the cat flap,' said Ben. 'But he did!'

Everyone jumped when the cat flap rattled. Jake stared at it, willing it to be Echo. But it wasn't him. It was Whiskers coming home.

'No luck?' Mum said, when they got back. Jake shook his head.

'But at least he's nearer now than he was,' Dad said. 'Frank's only a few miles away from us.'

Jake looked at the map and the red pins showing all the most likely sightings. As he did so, a tiny flicker of hope ran through him. The pins formed a rough triangle shape. Could his dad be right? Could Echo be trying to find his way home? If the pins were right, he was definitely heading in their direction.

Chapter 26

The railway station was very quiet when Echo went under the barrier and no one saw him. When the first train of the morning stopped and the passengers got out, Echo jumped up the steps and on to the train.

The conductor went down the platform, making sure all the carriage doors were properly closed, and then waved it on its way.

Echo tucked himself under a seat, but once the train was running he came out. Further down the carriage a woman was putting on her make-up and looking into a little compact mirror, but there was no one else about.

Echo hopped up on to a seat and looked out of the window as the train sped on, but he jumped off it again and lay in the bottom part of the luggage rack when the train pulled in at the next station. Each station they stopped at more people got on board as they headed into town for work and it wasn't long before Echo was spotted.

'Oh look . . .'

'Isn't he sweet?'

'What's it doing there?'

'Who's he with?'

But no one knew.

Echo went to sit with a man eating a sausage sandwich and when he was given some of it he wolfed it down. When the man got off at the next stop, Echo did too.

Outside the station he sniffed the air and smelt the delicious aroma of yesterday's noodles, fried chicken and curry not far away. Echo headed towards the scent of takeaways.

Boris, from Freddy's Fried Chicken, had stopped leaving water out for the little stray dog that used to visit them a while back. But as soon as he saw Echo he recognized him as the missing hearing dog and phoned the dog warden. She was only a few streets away.

'I'll be right there!'

Li couldn't believe it when he saw the little dog through the restaurant window.

'Hey, hey!' he waved excitedly.

Echo looked over at him and wagged his tail.

'Wait there!' Li shouted, holding out his palm in the same way that Jake did. Echo sat down and waited while Li ran to the kitchen.

'Call the dog warden and say Echo's come home,' he told the chef, as he spooned out a bowl of noodles and hurried out of the restaurant with them.

Echo skipped back when he saw him running. Li slowed to a leisurely walk so he wouldn't frighten the little dog.

'Look what I've got for you,' he said.

Echo watched Li set the bowl of noodles down on the ground and then came forward to eat them. Once the little dog was busily slurping up his free meal, Li tried to grab him. But before Li's fingers could even touch his fur Echo had darted away.

'OK,' Li said, holding his hands back in a gesture of surrender. 'No touching.'

Echo wagged his tail once as if he were agreeing and then stepped forward to finish the noodles.

Behind the little dog Li saw the dog warden creeping forward with her dog grasper – a pole with a loop at the end of it. Closer and closer she came. She was almost near enough to use the grasper when her shadow fell over the little dog. Echo looked round, his eyes opening wide when he saw the grasper, and he ran.

'Come back, Echo!' Li shouted after him. But Echo didn't stop.

As soon as the pelican crossing bleeps started, he raced across the road, then through the car park, across the churchyard, into the back garden of number 9 and under the broken gate of number 23.

He ran on across the grass until he came to the place where the old bridge had been, but it had disappeared. There was no way across the water unless he swam. He tentatively put his paw in the water and then took it out again.

But Jake was somewhere on the other side. It was the only way to reach him. Echo gave a whine and then jumped into the cold water. It was very deep and he sank under it, but instinctively splashed to the surface, gasping for air.

His paws moved fast under the water and at first he was only able to doggy-paddle in circles. But once he realized he wasn't going to sink he managed to calm down a little. His vision cleared and he swam across.

At the other side there was no way for him to get out. He started to panic as he struggled to get up the steep riverbank. He tried and failed and tried again, getting more desperate all the time.

''S OK, we'll help you,' said a familiar voice. The next moment the little dog was being lifted out of the river in a catch net.

'Best thing you've caught today, George,' the fisherman who was with him said, as Echo scrambled out of the net and vigorously shook himself.

'He reminds me of a dog I used to know. A dog called Bones, although his fur's a lot shorter than Bones's was,' George said, as he picked up his now soaked cheese-and-pickle sandwich.

Echo came forward and nudged George's hand and George stroked him.

'Well I never,' George said. 'Are you saying thank you?'

But even before George had finished speaking Echo was running on across the grass towards a bus stop. The bus that came along was very much like the one Echo had been on with Jake – even down to the driver's gingery beard.

'Assistance dogs travel free,' the driver said, as Echo slipped on board.

Echo sat on an empty seat, looking out of the window, as other passengers got on and off. He stood up and put his paws on the glass as they passed a school playground. A boy stood close to the fence, holding a ball. As the bus moved closer, Echo could see the boy more clearly. He whimpered and his heart started to beat very fast. It was Jake! He'd found him at last.

Echo barked and barked until the driver stopped and opened the doors. 'Go on then. Off you get.'

Echo jumped off the bus and ran along the pavement back to the school playground. But Jake wasn't there any more. The playground was empty.

Chapter 27

The children in Jake's class were presenting their dog projects. They'd already covered Romans and their dogs, police dogs, dog shows and puppy training.

A few children had done projects on dogs in wartime.

'A German shepherd from World War One went on to become a Hollywood movie star. His name was Rin Tin Tin . . .' Shula told everyone.

Amos didn't like writing much but he loved making things.

'I'm going to show you how to make a dog coat,' he said, holding up an old red sweatshirt.

'All you need is a sweatshirt or an old jumper and a pair of scissors and a dog to model it.'

He looked over at the large stuffed toy dog he'd put on the table and everyone laughed except for Jake.

Amos cut off one of the arms of the sweatshirt and then removed the wrist cuff too.

'It has to be wide enough for the dog's head to get through,' he said, picking up the toy dog. 'Then all you need to do is cut holes for the dog's front legs and cut the back to size and there you have it: a coat for a small dog, from the arm of a sweatshirt.'

'Thank you very much, Amos,' Miss Dawson said. 'I guess it would be suitable for a cat too?'

'Yes, miss, and you could make one for a hamster or a gerbil from a sock,' Amos told her. 'I don't have a dog but I do have a hamster. He's called Mr Munchy.'

This time Jake joined in when everyone laughed.

Just before lunch it was Chloe's turn to give her presentation.

'Did you know that people used to treat dogs like hamsters and put them on a wheel to run round and round to cook their food?' she asked the class.

Everyone shook their head.

'Well, they did. They were called turnspit dogs and there's a stuffed one in the Abergavenny Museum . . .'

'Yuck!'

'Yes – it was yuck, especially for those poor dogs.'

Tony was the first one to present his dog project after lunch.

'This little stray dog was called Rip,' he told everyone, showing a picture he'd stuck on a board. 'And he's credited with saving the lives of over a hundred people in

World War Two. The thing is, it doesn't matter what sort of dog you have. Or whether it's clever or brave or anything else. All dogs are stars to the people that love them.'

Echo crossed the playground and slipped in through the side door as the caretaker came out with a bag of rubbish. No one saw the little dog as he went down one corridor and up the next, his nose to the ground.

But, as he came to the end of the corridor and the glass swing doors, he lifted his head and sniffed the air. Sausages . . . and something else that was even more exciting: Jake's scent. Jake had been here and not long ago. The door was heavy for him to push so he went backwards and opened it with his bottom.

No one was in the hall now, but Echo found some sausage scraps that children had dropped on the floor and gobbled them up.

When one of the dinner ladies opened the swing door from the other side and propped it open with a metal food trolley, Echo slipped out of the hall, unseen. No one saw him until he went into the nursery classroom by mistake.

'A dog!' a little girl cried with delight.

The other children started squealing and running towards him with their hands outstretched. Echo quickly ducked back out again. Little children were scary!

'What dog?' the teacher said. She couldn't see anything. Nursery children tended to have very active imaginations. Yesterday they'd told her there was a dinosaur in the toilets.

'Gone now.'

Everyone clapped when Tony finished his presentation about search-and-rescue dog Rip. But Jake's stomach churned. It was his turn next.

'You've all done so well,' Miss Dawson said. 'I'm learning such a lot about dogs today. Now let's hear from you, Jake.'

The moment Jake had been dreading had arrived. He always hated standing up in front of everyone, apart from the time he'd told the class about sign language. That had been different because Echo was there and he'd felt like he could do anything.

Jake stood up and pressed his fingernails into the palms of his hands as he walked to the front. He was determined to give the best presentation that he possibly could. It was all about dogs like Echo and he wouldn't let him down.

'My project is about hearing dogs and all the amazing things they can do . . .' he said. His voice cracked but he kept on going anyway.

He told everyone about Helen Keller, a famous American lady who was both deaf and blind. She'd had a dog called Kamikaze-go or Go-Go for short.

'Whenever she went out on stage in public, she took her dog with her. I think Go-Go helped to give her confidence the same way having a hearing dog gives hundreds of deaf people confidence today. This was my hearing dog Echo's favourite toy,' Jake said, holding up the squeaky ball Tony had given him. 'He loved playing with it and making it squeak. Thank you for giving it to him, Tony.'

Tony looked up at Jake and smiled.

Jake squeezed the ball. And Echo, who was trotting down the corridor with his nose to the ground as he tried to pick up Jake's scent, heard the familiar squeak and raced towards the sound of it. He nudged the classroom door open and came bursting in, tail wagging.

Everyone started talking and shouting and laughing at once. But neither Echo nor Jake were listening.

'He came back!' Tony shouted.

'It's Echo!' squealed Chloe.

'But how . . .?'

'Echo!' Jake cried, as the little dog ran across the room, jumped up on to a desk and into his arms. He licked and licked his face as Jake laughed and cried.

'You came back,' Jake said, as he hugged the little dog. 'You came home.'

Chapter 28

'Echo came home,' Jake typed into the computer on the kitchen table.

Vicky was in the kitchen, making Echo some dog treats. Mum was on the phone to Dad.

'I'm turning the lorry round and coming home right now,' he said.

Then she was on the phone to Lenny at Helper Dogs: 'Yes, he just walked right into Jake's classroom!' She brushed away a tear and smiled, as she looked over at Jake and Echo together.

It wasn't easy for Jake to type with the little dog on his lap, but he didn't want to let him go ever again.

Within seconds of Jake's Facebook post, there were Like buttons pressed and comments posted.

'So pleased . . .'

'Congratulations!'

'Made my day.'

Jake's mum watched over his shoulder as more messages came in.

'We should have a party,' Jake said, and his mum's eyes widened in surprise. Jake had never wanted a party before, not even for his birthday.

'That's a great idea,' she agreed.

'A party for Echo,' said Jake as he stroked the little dog that was now fast asleep on his lap.

He started to make a list of everyone they should ask. Everyone who'd known Echo before he went missing and everyone who'd helped in the search to find him.

When his dad got home and saw how long the list was, he said maybe they should make the party a whole-day event at the weekend and everyone agreed.

'Are you sure you really want to invite all of your class?' he asked Jake.

Jake looked down at Echo and remembered how pleased the children had been when he came running into the classroom.

'Yes.'

'Jake should invite the whole school if he wants all of Echo's friends to be there,' Vicky said. 'Everyone at school loves him.'

The next morning more toys and balls and treats and home-made dog blankets started turning up for Echo. He already had two boxes full. But none of them could compete with the first squeaky ball that Tony had given Jake.

'Too many toys for you to play with or blankets to sleep on,' Jake told the little dog.

But then he had a good idea: there were other animals that might like these gifts very much.

On the day of the party, Dad and Jake strung balloons and lights all round the house. Vicky and her friends made a WELCOME HOME, ECHO! banner and had been busily preparing food since the night before with Echo as the chief taster.

Mum said it was just as well they'd started early because the house and garden were soon full to bursting with Echo's friends.

Everyone Jake knew from the deaf and hard-of-hearing club came and lots of the children from school did too.

'This is for Echo,' Amos said, and he gave Jake a dog coat that he'd made from the sleeve of his dad's old camo jacket.

'Thanks!' Jake said. It was too warm for Echo to wear now, but in the winter it would come in very handy. He was looking forward to his first Christmas with Echo and playing with him in the snow.

Bruno arrived with Heather and a welcome home card. There were almost a hundred other cards dotted round the house on windowsills already. Echo and the older dog touched noses and wagged tails before Bruno spotted Pippa and went to say hello to her too.

Li brought along a bucketful of Echo's favourite chicken fried noodles.

'Good for people and dogs,' he grinned as he set the bucket down. Echo gave him a pointed look.

Frank, Mary and their children came along too. They were delighted to see Waggy safe and sound.

'How's Whiskers?' Jake asked them.

'Comes and goes,' said Ben.

'But he's very lovely when he is visiting us,' Abby said.

'He's a cat who likes to do his own thing,' Frank added.

'Just like Jasper at the Helper Dogs centre,' Lenny said, giving Echo a stroke. He'd always had a suspicion that Jasper and Echo had gone exploring late at night when no one was around to see what they were up to. He'd never had any proof though, apart from the odd packet of treats being torn open by what looked like teeth.

Louise arrived with Hercules, and Echo wagged and wagged his tail at the sight of the old dog. As they sniffed at each other and touched noses, he could smell the scent of Gloria and the baby goats on Hercules' fur.

'Would you like these?' Jake asked her, pointing at the two boxes of blankets and dog toys that had been sent for Echo.

'Oh yes, please,' Louise said, looking inside.

A soft blue kangaroo toy fell out of one of the boxes and Hercules wagged his tail, went to pick it up, but stopped and looked up at Jake and then back at the toy as if he weren't sure if he could have it or not.

'Can he?' Jake asked Louise.

'Of course,' she smiled.

'Go on then,' Jake said to Hercules, pointing at the toy.

Hercules picked up the blue kangaroo gently between his teeth and went to lie down with it behind the sofa.

Echo alerted Jake that someone else was at the door; he'd forgotten none of his hearing helper dog training while he was away. When Jake opened it, he found Tony and Tara there.

Echo put his paw out to Tara and she bent down to give him a stroke.

'But I thought you were allergic to dogs,' Jake said. He'd assumed it would mean she didn't like them but apparently not.

'I'm fine if I take an antihistamine – which I'll need lots of when Tony gets his dog.' She grinned at Tony whose mouth was gaping open in surprise.

'What . . . but Mum and Dad . . . am I really?' he gasped.

'It's supposed to be a surprise for your birthday,' Tara said as Tony punched the air with happiness.

'We've got lots of puppies as well as all sorts of older dogs, big and small, looking for good homes at the rescue centre,' said Karen, who'd overheard them as she came in. She and the dog warden had brought three dogs that Echo had met while he was at the centre.

'Maybe we could have a dog or two at the hostel,' George said as Echo hopped up on to the sofa beside him. 'They make a place into a home.'

Jake, his dad and Echo had gone to the Fresh Start Hostel to invite all of Echo's old friends and Mr Cooper to the party. They were thrilled to see Echo home safe and sound and had brought a bone for him for old times' sake.

'Got a good home now, Bones,' George said as he stroked the little dog. 'Just like the rest of us.'

'Or we could have a cat,' Mr Cooper said to George as he gave Echo a stroke as well. 'A cat makes a home too.' He had always wanted a cat and one would be very welcome at the Fresh Start Hostel.

'Or both,' said Karen. 'We've so many dogs and cats desperate for a home at the rescue centre and lots of them get on very well together.'

Harvey nodded as he pulled a pencil from behind his ear and started to draw the dogs on the back of his paper plate.

'Where are we going?' Violet asked as the two nurses helped her into the home's minibus. And where was everyone else? The minibus only had her in it. She never usually went on a trip by herself.

'You've been invited to a party,' one of the nurses said.

'I have?' Violet asked in surprise. She hadn't been to a party, other than the small ones they had for the residents at the home, in years.

Jake looked out of the window and smiled as a minibus with SUNNY VIEW CARE HOME written on the side of it drew up outside the house. Two nurses helped a very, very old lady to get out.

'I can walk, you know,' Violet said.

But one of the nurses said it was safer for her if she stayed in the wheelchair for today.

'Safer?' said Violet. What sort of party was she going to? She'd never been to the house they were wheeling her up the path to in her life, or at least she didn't think she had.

When the front door opened, Violet couldn't believe her eyes. The little dog who'd saved her from the fire came running out, wagging his tail.

Violet patted her lap and he jumped up into it, nimble as a sprite, and licked her face.

'His name's Echo,' Jake told her. 'We're having a welcome home party for him.'

'Are you indeed? Well, I'm very glad to be invited,' Violet said. 'He saved me, you know.'

'The home sent Jake a Facebook message about it,' Vicky said, coming to the door too. 'He wanted to invite all of Echo's friends.'

Violet's eyes twinkled as she looked down at Echo. 'I'm very honoured to be called your friend,' she said.

'Come and have some cake,' said Jake's mum, and the nurses wheeled Violet, with Echo still on her lap, inside.

An hour later, Jake looked around at everyone and smiled. Dad was chatting to his lorry-driving friends, Frank and Bill. George and

Violet had their heads together and were laughing about something. Miss Dawson, Chloe and Louise were chatting about the possibility of a class project at the Home to Roost sanctuary. Vicky and Tara were comparing hairstyles. Mr Cooper was stroking Nora the Labrador, while Roxy, the chihuahua cross, munched on a home-made dog treat as Amos measured her for a dog coat, and Peter the collie played tug-tug with a Dog Lost volunteer and one of Echo's new toys.

Echo had so many friends and now they were Jake's friends too.

He squeezed the squeaky ball and Echo immediately looked up at him and wagged his tail as they headed out into the garden to play.

Acknowledgements

Echo's story has been an absolute pleasure to write, from the positive response to my initial idea until the final proof-copy read-through. During the writing of it, I was very fortunate to work with some amazing people, and spend time with many incredible animals. Special thanks must go to my wonderful editors Anthea Townsend and Carmen McCullough, editorial managers Samantha Stanton Stewart, Wendy Shakespeare and Nikki Sinclair, copy-editor Jane Tait, proofreaders Jennie Roman and Bea McIntyre, editorial assistant Natasha Brown, and cover designer Emily Smyth and illustrator Richard Jones. On the PR and marketing side there have been the brilliant Jessica Farrugia-Sharples and Hannah Maloco, as well as sales champions Tineke Mollemans and Kirsty Bradbury; and never forgetting my lovely agent, Clare Pearson of Eddison Pearson.

Books need readers and huge thanks to the booksellers, book clubs, librarians and teachers who've been such advocates of my books. And even bigger thanks to the children who've read them and sent letters and emails to say how much they've enjoyed them. ☺

Researching hearing dogs, both those that have been formally trained and otherwise, and seeing the work they do and the difference they make, has been a fascinating and a joyous delight!

I wear hearing aids myself and tried teaching Bella how to find my mobile phone. She's almost grasped running to it when it rings, but she would really rather chase her ball or be swimming in the river. However, she has taught herself that a good way to wake me up when I'm sleeping, and don't have my hearing aids in, is to give my arm a nudge with her nose.

The charity Dog Lost has been part of our lives ever since we found an old dog wandering along a busy main road and took her home with us. Fortunately, with Dog Lost's and the police's help (she wasn't microchipped), we were able to reunite her with her family over two hundred miles away. The volunteers at Dog Lost do an incredible job and whenever I see on their website that a dog's been reunited with its family it makes my day.

Some dogs, of course, don't have a home to return to, and as Karen in the book says there are so many wonderful dogs and cats waiting for their forever home in rescue centres around the country. The animals at Thrift Farm were a huge help when I was writing the farm sanctuary scenes – especially the lively baby goats.

In 2015 I was invited to start off a story for children to continue for the PDSA children's writing competition 'Pet Tales'. The winner, Francesca, has two Border terriers, Roxy and Eddie, who I'm sure would have loved playing with Echo. Jasper, the Helper Dogs cat in the book, is actually an RSPCA rescue cat who loves dogs, and appears thanks to a kind donation to Authors for Nepal.

Thanks as always must go to my husband who brought Bella along to schools to meet lots of children this year. Our own dogs, Traffy and Bella, are a constant source of writing inspiration. They very much enjoyed being the official taste testers for the dog treats Jake and Vicky make in the book. Some of the recipes they tried can be found below.

Dog-treat Recipes

There are lots of great dog-treat recipes available to choose from, but a basic one I often use is Traffy's Cheese Stars. Even if you don't measure the ingredients exactly, it will still work, and it doesn't matter if you or your dog tastes it when it's still raw.

I usually make mine using either cheese or easy-peasy home-made peanut butter. All you need to do is blend together a few handfuls of shelled peanuts and a couple of teaspoons of groundnut oil for one to three minutes. It tastes extra delicious and creamy for both humans and dogs! If you do use peanut butter from a jar, make sure it doesn't list xylitol as one of the ingredients as it's very bad for dogs.

Cheesy Marmite treats are delicious too – with just a little bit of Marmite as it's salty. I'm sure you'll be able to think of lots more. Let me know if you come up with a good recipe because I'm sure my dogs would love to try it too. ☺

Traffy's Cheese Stars

(These are also irresistible to humans.)

You will need:

200 g flour
30 ml water (add more if necessary)
60 ml olive oil
100 g Cheddar cheese

How to make them:

1. Set the oven to 180°C or gas mark 4, so it can heat up while you're making the mixture.
2. Mix all the ingredients together in a bowl to make a dough.
3. Roll it out as thin as you can. The thinner the dough is, the

crunchier the treats will be. Use a star pastry cutter (or any shape cutter, or just squash a ball of dough into a flat circle if you don't have a cutter).

4. Place the treats on a baking sheet lined with parchment paper or lightly greased silver foil so they don't stick, and pop them in the oven to bake.

5. Check after ten minutes. The treats should be lightly browned.

6. You can put the treats back inside the oven and turn the oven off now. They'll get crunchier as they cool. But I don't usually do this because there are two pairs of doggy eyes staring pointedly at me as soon as I take the treats out of the oven.

7. Wait until the treats have cooled down and enjoy. ☺

Bella's Peanut-butter Bones

These use the same method and most of the same ingredients as Traffy's Cheese Stars – only you'll be using peanut butter instead of cheese this time. I find I need a little bit more water with these than with the cheese ones.

Bella was in the kitchen with me when I cooked up my last batch of dog treats. She made her funny little grumbly *mmm-mmm* sounds as I took them out of the oven. Once they were cool enough, I tried to see which she liked most, peanut butter or cheese, by offering her one of each and seeing which one she picked first. But she seemed to like them both the same!

You will need:

200 g flour (any sort)
60 ml water

30 ml olive oil

2 tbsp (or more) peanut butter

How to make them:

1. Set the oven to 180°C or gas
   mark 4.
2. Mix all the ingredients together in a
   bowl to make a dough and roll it out.
   (If you don't have a rolling pin, you
   could just squash the dough as flat as
   you can with your hands.)
3. Use a bone-shaped pastry cutter
   to make the treats, place them on
   a baking tray and cook for ten
   minutes. (If you don't have a
   pastry cutter, you could break the
   dough up into little balls or tear off
   little bits instead and place them on
   the baking tray. Most dogs won't
   mind if their treats are a bit
   misshapen!)

Finally, if you don't like baking, here's a recipe for peanut-butter oat treats that you don't even need to turn the oven on for.

No-need-to-cook Peanut-butter Bites

You will need:

50 g oats
1 tbsp peanut butter
50 ml water

How to make them:

1. Mix all the ingredients together in a bowl (the amounts don't have to be too exact).
2. Roll the mixture into small balls and put on a plate.
3. Put the plate in the fridge to set – or eat them there and then, as Bella prefers to do, because she doesn't like to be kept waiting. ☺

Turn the page for an extract from

The Runaways

by Megan Rix

AVAILABLE NOW

www.meganrix.com

Chapter 1

Harvey always wore the turquoise ruff around his furry black-and-white neck for the show. So when he saw the baby elephant heading towards him, intent on pulling it off as she'd managed to do the day before, he skittered away from her before she got a chance.

Tara gave a trumpeting *squee* as she headed after the Border collie across the elephant tent. But Harvey was too old and wily to be caught by a two-year-old elephant and he hid under the oversized props they sometimes used in the act. Tara knelt down and stretched out her trunk as far as it would go, but hard as she tried she couldn't reach him. Finally she gave a trumpet of frustration, headed back to her mother, Shanti, and had some milk instead.

Drink over, the baby elephant watched from the other side of the tent as fifteen-year-old Albert, dressed in a turquoise 'Arabian Nights' elephant trainer's costume, carefully combed his hair in front of the full-length mirror. Harvey poked his pointy nose under one of the props and watched Tara watching Albert.

Deep in thought, Albert put the comb back in his pocket and didn't pay attention to the little elephant as she pottered over to him.

Tara stuck out her trunk and ruffled his just-combed fair hair.

'Tara!' he said, pulling out the comb again and quickly smoothing his hair back down. 'You can be a little minx sometimes!'

Tara gave a joyful *squee* that sounded almost like a giggle. Not sorry at all. As soon as he'd finished combing his hair, she went to mess it up again, but this time her mother stopped her with her trunk and a warning noise.

Albert felt sorry for the elephants. In the wild they'd be able to wander wherever they liked. Tara would have other elephants to play with and probably a watering hole or a river to splash in rather than the bucket of water that was all he could manage to give her. He always treated the elephants with kindness, unlike some trainers he'd heard about. But, nevertheless, they spent most of their days and nights tied up in their tent, apart from when they were performing for the public in the big top.

He really couldn't blame Tara for wanting to play or for being mischievous. She was bored. He knew that the circus wasn't the right place for the elephants to be, but he tried to make it the best place for them that he could. Maybe their new home would be better. He hoped so.

'Here, Shanti, let's put this on you,' Albert said, picking up the multicoloured headdress the Asian elephant wore during the show. It had been made especially for her and had her name embroidered across the star in the centre.

Shanti bowed her giant head so he could tie the headdress behind her ears. She'd been part of circus life from the time she was five years old and she was now twenty-two.

'You look beautiful,' he told the sweet-natured, gentle elephant as he pressed his face into her warm, rough skin and ran his hand down her trunk. Shanti made a soft rumbling sound.

Tara, however, did not help Albert like her mother had done. As soon as she saw him pick up her own much smaller headdress she turned round so her bottom was facing him instead of her face. When Albert walked round to the front of her she made a noise that sounded very much like a giggle and turned round the other way.

'Come on, Tara, you know you have to wear it,' he told her. He didn't want them to be late for their very last show.

But Tara only shook her head and backed away as he stepped towards her. They'd played this game before.

Harvey came out from under the props and looked from one to the other, his tail wagging.

'Hmm,' said Albert, putting his hand in his pocket and acting as if he didn't care a bit what Tara did. He pulled out an apple, one of Tara's favourite treats, and Tara stretched out her trunk, wanting to take the apple from him.

Albert looked at the apple in one hand and then he looked at Tara's headdress in his other hand and waggled it. Tara knew exactly what she needed to do if she wanted the apple.

She stood quietly in front of Albert and let him put on her headdress with her name embroidered across the star like her mum's.

'That's a good elephant,' Albert said, giving her a stroke. Tara's skin was much less rough and a lot more furry than Shanti's. She even had a tuft of fur on the top her head that gave her an impish look. It matched her personality, he thought.

Albert bit into the apple and shared the bitten pieces between the little elephant and Shanti. Harvey barked and nudged Albert with his nose.

'Don't worry, I haven't forgotten you.' Albert smiled at the old dog. 'There's a bone for you, but not till after the show.'

Albert checked himself one last time in the mirror before they left the tent. It was the last time he'd wear the sparkling turquoise elephant trainer's outfit before he set off for the front. The last time for, well he didn't exactly know quite how long, that he, Shanti, Tara and Harvey would perform together.

When the war started in August 1914 his father had said it would be over by Christmas.

Everyone thought it would be done and dusted in a few months. But it was now September 1917 and the war was still going on, only his dad wasn't around any more to see the end of it. Thinking about how much he missed him made Albert feel sad. At least his father had got to see Tara being born before he died and Albert was glad about that. It had always been very important to his dad that Shanti was happy and no mum could have been happier with her baby than Shanti was. Not many people get to see a newborn elephant, and Tara had looked so sweet as she took her first wobbly steps while Shanti stood protectively over her. For a long time she hid under her mum's tummy whenever she was scared or worried about anything.

'But you don't seem to be scared of much these days, do you? More like full of mischief and fun!' he told the baby elephant as she stretched out her trunk towards his head and he ducked back from her before she could mess up his hair again.

The band started to play, which meant the matinee audience must be seated. It was time to go on.

Albert still felt nervous before each perform-ance even though he knew no one was really watching him. The audience only had eyes for the elephants, and that was just the way it should be, in Albert's opinion. Shanti and Tara were the most beautiful, majestic and just downright magical creatures he could ever imagine, and he wanted to share their grace with everyone.

Harvey pushed his head under Albert's hand and Albert stroked him.

'Come on then, one last show. Let's make it a good one,' Albert said, as they headed for the big top. 'Tails!' he instructed, and Tara held on to Shanti's tail as she was supposed to do. Shanti, as always, took the lead, with Harvey bringing up the rear.

The band was playing a new tune now.

Harvey panted as he waited to go into the ring.

'Wait for it,' Albert told him, as he looked round the tent flap at the afternoon's audience.

Those who'd paid the most for their seats got to sit on the comfortable maroon velvet padded chairs at the front. But there were only two people sitting in those seats today. A middle-aged woman with her brown hair tied in a bun, and a suited man in a hat sitting beside her.

The rest of the audience at Whitehaven was pitifully small. Maybe twelve in total on the cheaper bench seats. Six of those were voluntary nurses in uniform, plus a soldier and his girlfriend and three children with their mum.

Albert bit his bottom lip. Not enough people to keep an elephant in cabbages; certainly not enough to pay a whole circus crew. Not that they had a proper crew any more. Most of the younger men had enlisted already. The circus was on its knees and couldn't go on. This matinee wasn't just the last show for Albert, the elephants and Harvey. It was the last show for everyone else in the circus too.

The ringmaster, Jedediah Lewis, was in the centre of the ring. He whisked off his top hat, raised it in the air, and shouted, 'And now for your delight and entertainment, at great expense, all the way from the jungle . . .'

As the first note of the popular 'Royal Decree' march was banged out by the band, Harvey gave a small whine and put out his paw.

Albert pulled back the tent flap and the three animals ran into the circus ring. As Albert went past the maroon chairs, he heard the woman say:

'Now we're in for a treat.'

'Whatever you say, Beatrix,' the man told her as he checked his pocket watch.

The animals paraded round until the music changed to a tinkling lullaby and then, quick as a flash, Harvey jumped into the pram that

Albert pushed into the ring. Shanti curled her trunk round the oversized handle, and as 'Rock-a-bye Baby' continued to play she rocked the pram back and forth as if she were lulling a baby to sleep. Meanwhile, Tara took the giant-sized baby's bottle that Albert held out to her. It was filled with water that she tipped into her mouth.

Albert glanced over as the scant audience *ooohed*, *aaahed* and clapped. His eyes widened as he watched a red-faced, broken-nosed man sit down at the back of the bench seats. What on earth was Carl from Cullen's Circus doing here? There was bad blood between Albert's family and Cullen's Circus where Carl worked as the elephant trainer. Shanti had come from there and the last time Albert's father had seen Carl he'd been so angry with his cruel treatment of her that there had almost been a fight. But what was Carl doing at the Lewis Brothers' show?

Read all of Megan Rix's wonderful wartime animal stories . . .

'If you love Michael Morpurgo, you'll enjoy this'
Sunday Express

AVAILABLE NOW

www.meganrix.com